"*Eu quero voce...* I want you," Zac growled. **"*Why* is that wrong?"**

"I didn't say it was wrong!" Freddie gasped. "I said it was wrong to try and use money to tempt me."

Zac extended a hand to wind long brown fingers very slowly through the fall of her hair, his every hunting instinct on high alert. "But you already want me," he contended with devastating assurance. "You wanted me the first time you saw me, so why are we still arguing about it?"

Zac tugged her closer and bent his arrogant dark head lower and lower until he finally found her mouth, where the sultry sweet taste of her released a surge of such powerful lust he trembled with it.

Freddie had never ever had a kiss of that magnitude. Admittedly, life had ensured that she had not had the opportunity to have many kisses, but when she got her arms wrapped round Zac's neck for the merest fraction of a second she felt as if she never ever wanted to let go because she felt safe, safe for the first time since she had lost her parents, safe as if nothing bad could ever happen to her again. And that unholy kiss... All of a sudden, Freddie wanted what she had never wanted before.

Vows for Billionaires

His heir, in exchange for his ring!

Angel Valtinos, Prince Vitale Castiglione and Zac Da Rocha have more than just a father in common—these three billionaires have reputations for ruthless command! No women have ever breached their defenses. But they're about to be faced with unexpected consequences...

To legitimize their legacies, they must strike a deal. But will a vow be enough for the mothers of their children—or will they need passion to walk down the aisle?

The Secret Valtinos Baby

Castiglione's Pregnant Princess

Da Rocha's Convenient Heir

Available now!

Lynne Graham

—

DA ROCHA'S
CONVENIENT HEIR

 HARLEQUIN PRESENTS®

Recycling programs
for this product may
not exist in your area.

ISBN-13: 978-1-335-41940-8

Da Rocha's Convenient Heir

First North American publication 2018

Printed in U.S.A.

Lynne Graham was born in Northern Ireland and has been a keen romance reader since her teens. She is very happily married to an understanding husband who has learned to cook since she started to write! Her five children keep her on her toes. She has a very large dog who knocks everything over, a very small terrier who barks a lot and two cats. When time allows, Lynne is a keen gardener.

Books by Lynne Graham

Harlequin Presents

Bought for the Greek's Revenge
The Sicilian's Stolen Son

Vows for Billionaires

The Secret Valtinos Baby
Castiglione's Pregnant Princess

Wedlocked!

His Queen by Desert Decree
Claimed for the Leonelli Legacy

Brides for the Taking

The Desert King's Blackmailed Bride
The Italian's One-Night Baby
Sold for the Greek's Heir

Christmas with a Tycoon

The Italian's Christmas Child
The Greek's Christmas Bride

Visit the Author Profile page
at Harlequin.com for more titles.

CHAPTER ONE

ZAC DA ROCHA, the Brazilian billionaire, powered towards his father's office on long muscular legs. He was in a rare state of surprise because his stuffy, rigidly formal half-brother, Vitale, the Crown Prince of Lerovia, had just matched the facetious bet Zac had made him earlier that morning. Zac enjoyed yanking Vitale's chain but he had not expected a retaliation. He raked his hand impatiently through the long, luxuriant dark hair falling onto his broad shoulders and grinned with sudden appreciation, flashing perfect white teeth in the process. Maybe Vitale wasn't such a narrow-minded bore after all. Maybe he had more in common with his half-sibling than he had assumed.

As quickly as that idea occurred to him, Zac suppressed it again because he wasn't looking for a family connection. He had never had a family. He had looked up his long-lost father, Charles Russell, out of pure curiosity and had lingered on the edge of the family circle out of pure badness, thoroughly entertained by the immediate animosity of his two half-brothers, Vitale and Angel. The emergence of a third son had shocked and unsettled them and Zac had made little effort to foster a sibling relationship. But then what the hell did he know about blood ties? He had never had a brother or a sister and, what was more, he had had a mother he had seen only once a year if he was lucky, a stepfather who hated him and a birth father whose identity he had only discovered the year before when his mother had finally told him the truth she had long withheld because she was dying.

Yet when it came to his birth father, for once in his life he had landed lucky, Zac conceded grudgingly, because he actually *liked* Charles Russell. Zac was more accustomed to people who tried to use him and he trusted very few people. His light grey-blue eyes hardened. Fabulously rich from birth and raised like a little prince, surrounded by fawning servants, Zac was very cynical about human nature. But from their first meeting, Charles had taken a genuine interest in his third and youngest adult son, despite the fact that, at twenty-eight and six feet four inches tall, that son was already a man grown.

After only a few hours in the older man's radius, Zac had realised how much better he would have done had his mother, Antonella, chosen to stay with Charles rather than choosing to marry the playboy fortune hunter, Afonso Oliveira, the love of his mother's life. Unhappily, while being engaged to Antonella, Afonso had got cold feet and dumped her for several weeks. Heartbroken, Antonella had succumbed to a rebound affair with Charles, then in the process of divorcing a wife who had been cheating on him throughout their marriage with another woman. But then, Afonso had returned to Antonella to ask for her forgiveness and Antonella had followed her heart. When soon after the wedding she had realised she was pregnant, she had fervently hoped that she carried Afonso's child and had refused to acknowledge that Zac might not be her husband's son. Sadly, for all of them, Zac's very rare blood group had become a ticking time bomb in his mother's marriage.

As Zac strode into his father's office he was rewarded by an immediate smile of warm welcome and acceptance. He might be a tattooed guy clad in jeans and biker boots with diamond studs in his ear but Charles, the grey-haired older man who greeted him in an immaculate business suit, treated him the exact same as his other sons.

'I did think of putting on a suit to surprise the brothers,' Zac murmured deadpan, his strikingly light eyes glittering with self-mockery against his bronzed skin. 'But I didn't want them to think I was conforming to expectations or competing.'

'No fear of that, I think.' Charles laughed, wrapping his arms round his very tall and vociferously different son in a whole-hearted embrace before stepping back. 'Any news yet from your lawyers about your chances of breaking the trust?'

The internationally renowned Quintal da Rocha diamond mines had been locked into a trust by Zac's great-great-grandfather to protect the family heritage. Since his mother's death, Zac had been in possession of the income from the mines but he would not have the right to control the extensive Da Rocha business empire until he produced an heir of his own. It was an iniquitous arrangement, which had sentenced previous generations to a deeply dysfunctional family life, and Zac had long been determined to break the cycle. Sadly, the answer his legal team had given him was not the one he had sought.

He could not be truly independent or free until he had met the terms of the trust one way or another. Hedged by restrictions throughout childhood and adolescence, he had railed against the trust when he had finally understood how it would limit him. He was the last da Rocha and he enjoyed enormous wealth but until he fulfilled the conditions imposed by that trust he had no more rights than a child to control the diamond mines and the vast business empire built on the back of their profits. He felt sidelined, powerless and dispossessed by his current weak position and there was little he would not have given to be free of it.

'My lawyers tell me that if I marry and *fail* over time to produce a child they think there would be little problem breaking the trust,' Zac revealed grimly, his chiselled cheekbones taut. 'But that would take years and I'm not prepared to wait for years to run what is mine by right of blood.'

Charles expelled his breath in a slow hiss. 'So, you're going to get married,' he assumed.

Zac frowned. 'I don't need to get married,' he countered. 'Any heir will meet the terms of the trust, boy or girl, legitimate or otherwise.'

'Legitimate would be better,' Charles protested quietly.

'But the ensuing divorce settlement would cost me a fortune,' Zac responded with resounding practicality. 'Why marry when I don't have to?'

'For the child's sake,' Charles supplied with a grimace. 'To protect the child from growing up as both you and your mother did, isolated from normal life.'

Zac parted his lips as though he was about to say something and then thought better of it, swinging restively away. His grandfather had found himself married to a barren wife. He had then impregnated a maid in the household, who had given birth to Zac's mixed-race mother. Antonella had been whisked away to be raised at a remote ranch, separated from her mother and never acknowledged by her aristocratic father once her arrival had refuelled his wealthy lifestyle. She had been an heiress but one from the kind of humble background the rich and sophisticated delighted in despising.

Initially, Zac's stepfather, Afonso, had assumed that Zac was *his* child and he had married Antonella, willing to turn a blind eye to her embarrassing background if he could share her riches. When Zac was three years old, however, his need for a blood transfusion after an accident had roused Afonso's suspicions about his parentage and the truth had emerged. Zac still remembered Afonso screaming at him that he was not his child and that he was 'a dirty, filthy half-breed'. After that fallout, Zac had been transported to the ranch to be raised by staff, out of sight and out of mind while Antonella worked on repairing the marriage that meant so much to her.

'He's my husband and he comes first. He *has* to come first,' Antonella had told Zac when he'd asked to go home with her after one of her fleeting visits to see him.

'I love him. You can't come to Rio. It will only put Afonso in a bad mood,' she had argued vehemently years later with tears in her beautiful eyes.

Yet Afonso had enjoyed countless affairs during his marriage while Antonella struggled to give him a child of his own, suffering innumerable miscarriages and finally the premature birth that had claimed her life when she was already well beyond the age when child bearing was considered safe. Afonso had not even come to the funeral and Zac had buried his weak-willed but lovely mother with a stone where his heart should've been and the inner conviction that he would never ever marry or fall in love, because love had only taught his mother to reject and neglect her only child.

'I married two very beautiful women, neither of whom was the least maternal,' his father, Charles, told him heavily, pulling Zac suddenly back into the present. 'Angel and Vitale paid the price with unhappy home lives. Right now you're at a crossroads and you have a choice, Zac. Give marriage a chance. Choose a woman who at least *wants* a child and give her the opportunity, with your support, to be a normal mother to that child. Children need two parents because bringing up a child is tough. I did the best I could after the divorces but I wasn't around enough to make a big difference in my sons' lives.'

It was quite a speech and it came from the heart; Zac almost groaned out loud because he could see where his father was coming from. Although marrying would cost him millions when it inevitably broke down, that legal framework *would* provide a certain stability for the child. It would be a stability that he had never enjoyed but then, unlike his grandfather, he had always planned to be involved in his child's life, hadn't he? Even so, if he wasn't *married* to the mother of his child, his freedom to be involved would be dictated by her. He already knew those facts, had worked through all possible options with his legal team and preferred not to think about those facts because they only depressed him. After all, the odds of him having a good relationship with his child's mother were slim, he reflected impatiently.

Women *always* wanted more from Zac than he was prepared to give…more time, more money, more attention. But all he had ever wanted from a woman was sex and once that was over, he was done. He was an unashamed player, who had never been in a real relationship, who had never pledged fidelity and who could not bear the sensation of being caged by anyone or anything. In many ways, he had been caged most of his life, raised on a remote ranch before being placed in a stiflingly strict boarding school run by the clergy and forced to follow endless rules. He hadn't known a moment of true freedom until he reached university and it was hardly surprising that he had then gone off the rails for a while. In fact, it had been a few years before he got back on track and completed his business degree.

And what had brought him back? The discovery that at heart he was a da Rocha and that he couldn't run away from his birthright. A workers' dispute in which he was powerless to intervene on their behalf had persuaded him to start attending business meetings and, although he still couldn't legally call the shots, he had discovered that the directors were very wary of making an outright enemy of him. Like Zac, they looked to the future.

'How long will you be away?' Charles prompted,

aware that Zac was leaving London to check out the diamond mines in South Africa and Russia.

Zac shrugged. 'Five…maybe six weeks. I've a lot to catch up on but I'll stay in touch.'

Leaving his father's office, Zac headed back to The Palm Tree, the small, exclusive and very opulent hotel he had bought in preference to an apartment of his own. His thoughts immediately turned in a more frivolous direction, escaping with relief from the serious ramifications of his father's sage advice. He had bet his brother that he couldn't find an ordinary woman and pass her off as his socialite partner at the royal ball to which he had also been invited. Unsurprisingly, Vitale, who didn't have a humorous bone in his entire body, had been unamused by the challenge but, on emerging from his meeting with their father earlier, Vitale had startled Zac by not only accepting the bet but also by making his own. And what had followed had had very much an 'own goal' feel for Zac…

Remember that little blonde waitress who wanted nothing to do with you last week and accused you of harassment? Bring her to the ball acting all lovelorn and clingy and suitably polished up and you have a deal on the bet.

Freddie? Lovelorn and clingy? That was the challenge to end all challenges when he couldn't even get her to join him for a drink! His even white teeth clenched hard in frustration. Zac had never before

met with an outright rejection from a woman and it
had infuriated him, his innate need to compete making him persist. But Freddie had interpreted per-
sistence as harassment and had burst into tears in
Vitale's presence, a fiercely embarrassing moment
that had frozen Zac where he'd sat in all male horror at what he had unleashed on himself in a public place. Even more gallingly, Vitale had stepped
straight in to defuse the scene with all the right
soothing words until another waitress had arrived
to rescue them. But then that was Vitale, all smooth,
slippery and refined in a way Zac was distinctly
aware that he himself was not. The most formative
years of Zac's life had been the dropout years when
he had belonged to a biker club, not rubbing shoulders with the rich and sophisticated in polite society.

In polite society, Zac was mobbed by women
seduced by his great wealth and he avoided such
women like the plague, well aware that they would've
been equally enthusiastic even if he were old, bald
and unpleasant. That he was none of those things
simply made him more of a target. He had loved the
male brotherhood in the club, the easy acceptance,
the loyalty and the complete lack of rules that had
enabled him to be himself. He had enjoyed women
equally happy to enjoy him in bed, women without an agenda, only looking for pleasure. But after
a while, even that had got old and as soon as the
Brazilian media had discovered his hideout and ex-

posed the story of the billionaire biker boy, he had moved regretfully on, knowing that phase of his life was over.

He revelled now in the anonymity of his life in London and had avoided his siblings' social gatherings out of a strong desire to preserve it. Spoiled, privileged young women with cut-glass accents didn't do it for him because they saw him as a prize trophy to be won. He had met with more sincerity and honesty in people his brothers would probably snobbishly deem to be vulgar and uneducated. And even conservative Vitale had conceded that Freddie was a real looker.

Zac only knew that he had never wanted a woman with such instantaneous lust. Lust at first glance, he conceded grimly, thinking it ironic that out of all the many women who wanted him back his libido had had to focus on one who not only did not want him, but also actively appeared to dislike him. He couldn't accept that he had done or said anything to incite that reaction from her and the injustice had outraged him, encouraging his damaging determination to change her attitude. *Meu Deus*, after her outburst, he would scarcely be looking in that direction again, which meant that Vitale had won the bet outright and as the loser he would have to hand over his cherished sports car. Exasperation and growing annoyance gripped him. He would now be gone for weeks in any case.

One last try...

When he got back to London next month, what would he have to lose? He could attempt outright bribery, Zac decided with sudden savage cynicism... *use* the power of money to persuade for once in his life. Freddie had refused his first generous tip and then had just as swiftly changed her mind and accepted it, he recalled with a sceptical curl of his full sensual mouth. She would turn out to be like every other woman he had ever met: she would surrender for money. After all, she wasn't working all day on her feet as a waitress for fun.

Freddie was having a dream about a man with eyes the colour of crushed ice, a wealth of silky blue-black hair and a full sensual mouth.

It was a wonderful dream until a little hand shook her arm and a little voice said, 'Bekfast? Auntie Fred...*bekfast*?' while one warm little body pushed for space in her single bed and another warm little body crawled up over the top of her.

With a groan, Freddie woke up and checked her alarm in case she had slept in. Some hope of that with her nephew and niece around, she thought ruefully, with three-year-old Eloise pinning her up against the wall and ten-month-old Jack lying on top of her in a happy baby sprawl.

'You *don't* lift Jack out of his cot,' she told her

niece for the tenth time. 'He could get hurt. It's not safe if I'm still asleep—'

'You wake now,' Eloise pointed out cheerfully as Freddie scrambled over her with Jack in her arms and went to change him.

A vague recollection of her dream flushed her triangular face and her soft mouth tightened, her brown eyes sparkling with self-loathing. Loser alert, loser alert, she chanted inside her head in exasperation. Eloise and Jack's father, Cruz, had been a very good-looking guy as well, beautifully dressed and polite, but he had turned out to be a terrifyingly violent drug dealer and a pimp. Her older sister, Lauren, had died of a drug overdose within days of Jack's birth, utterly destroyed by the man she had loved, who had not only refused to acknowledge his children but had also so far escaped paying a single penny towards their support.

Zac whatever-his-name-was might not be either beautifully dressed *or* polite, but he had been staying for weeks in the very expensive penthouse suite in the exclusive hotel where she worked in the bar and, although he had been gone for over a month now, the suite was apparently being held for his return. How the heck was he affording that when as far as she could see he didn't engage in any normal form of work? He also mixed with some very flash, international, business-suited men. He was dubious and up to no good, of course he was, she told herself angrily, furious that the Brazilian had invaded her dreams. It had been bad enough, she acknowledged, when she'd had to see him every day in the bar. And now that he was gone, why hadn't she completely forgotten about him?

It was even more weird that he had shown such an interest in her in the first place, she reflected irritably. She had seen how attractive he was to women while she worked. Zac wasn't a mere babe magnet, more a babe tornado. She had seen desperate women do everything but strip in front of him in an effort to gain his attention. They nudged up to him at the bar, tripped nearby, tried to strike up conversations and buy him drinks. And he acted as if they didn't exist, behaving like a blind celibate monk in their radius. Weird and suspicious, *right*?

After all, Freddie *knew* she wasn't a show-stopper. She was way too undersized to be one. Barely five feet tall and slender, with only a very modest amount of curves. She had dark blonde hair that fell halfway to her waist and plain brown eyes. So why would a guy with Zac's attributes chase a waitress unless he was a weirdo? Or some kind of user who assumed she would be stupid enough to fall for whatever nefarious purpose he had in mind? Well, no, Freddie had never been stupid and she knew how to look after herself, particularly after having spent years watching her late sister make the very worst decisions possible.

Freddie made breakfast for the children quietly, striving not to wake up her aunt, Claire, who had come home in the early hours. Claire, her late mother's youngest sister, was only six years older than twenty-two-year-old Freddie, so they had never had the traditional auntie/niece connection, being far too close in age for that, but they had always got on well. Even so, just at present Freddie was worried about the other woman's mood. Claire was being evasive and quiet, not to mention going out a lot and using a babysitter without ever talking about where she was going. Freddie believed in respecting Claire's privacy but, at the same time, she couldn't help worrying herself sick that their little 'family' arrangement was somehow at risk.

At Freddie's instigation, Claire had applied to foster the kids after Freddie was turned down for the job. That had been after Lauren's death when the welfare services had wanted to remove the kids from Freddie's care and put them into a foster home with strangers. Freddie had been deemed too young and inexperienced to take charge of the children she had been looking after from birth—for that was the unlovely truth about her late sister's parenting skills. Lauren's world had had only two focuses: drugs and her violent, threatening boyfriend. Freddie had long been the only person available to care for Eloise and Jack while trying at the same time to dissuade her sister from her worst excesses.

And there she had failed abysmally, she conceded sadly, having found it impossible either to get Lauren off drugs or to persuade her to break up with Cruz. Grief still filled her when she thought of the loving, light-hearted big sister she had grown up with and clung to in foster care. Their parents had died in a car crash when Freddie was ten and there had been no relatives willing to take them in. Five years older, Lauren had been more like a little substitute mother than a big sister, at least, *until* she had fallen under Cruz's influence and every rule had been broken, every moral flouted, every evil permitted. Freddie had been stuck in the middle of all that horror from the day of Eloise's birth, knowing that if she moved out her niece would be lucky to survive that chaotic household where only constant vigilance protected the weak and vulnerable. Claire had urged her to walk away and turn her back but she had loved Eloise too much to do that.

So, when Claire had generously agreed to apply to be the kids' foster carer even though she wasn't really 'a kiddy person', as she put it, the agreement had been that Freddie would continue doing the lion's share of the childcare. That meant that Freddie stayed home days to see to the children and worked nights in a bar, having readied the kids for bed before she left Claire's tiny terraced home. Claire had confessed herself content to live off the foster-care

payments but Freddie had had to find work to bring
in some extra money.

And during Zac's stay at the hotel, his tips had
virtually doubled Freddie's earnings. He had rou-
tinely tossed her two fifty-pound notes every time
she served him and the first time, aware of his personal interest, she had taken umbrage and tossed
them back, telling him she wasn't for sale, only to
be ambushed by another waitress who had angrily
reminded her that their tips went into a communal
pot, so she had had to go back to Zac's table and
apologise and pick up the discarded notes.

His unsought generosity had, however, reclothed
Eloise and Jack, put some very nice meals on the
table and now that little gold pile was almost gone it
was time for a treat, she thought, determined to start
being more positive and stop worrying about Claire,
who, ultimately, would do what she wanted to do regardless of what anyone else wanted. Equally, why
was she beating herself up about a stupid dream?
Fantasies were harmless and, in the flesh, Zac was
decidedly a fantasy, a traffic-stoppingly beautiful
man whom women stood still to study until they rec-
ollected themselves and, blushing, moved on.

Of course, Freddie had done worse several
weeks earlier when she had lost her temper with
Zac and then burst into floods of tears. The stress
of two sleepless nights with Jack running a fever
had smashed all her defences flat. Claire had been

so irritable about his crying disturbing her sleep and Freddie had been so exhausted, she had simply cracked down the middle and snapped when Zac had merely put a hand on her spine to steady her when she'd wobbled in the very high heels she had to wear for work. She had learned to be very averse to men touching her while she was living with her sister, whose home had overflowed with untrustworthy men. She had developed the habit of maintaining rigid boundaries and it had come back to haunt her at the worst possible moment.

But then, although she had been forced to apologise for the scene she had made to retain her job, she had still believed her hysterical outburst couldn't have happened to a more suitable person. Zac's very first words to her, after all, had been unrepeatably dirty and blunt, an invitation to spend the night with him but not one couched in polite or acceptable terms. She had had many such invites before but he was the first who had ever employed that kind of language to her face and she had felt soiled by it, besmirched by the simple fact she had to wear denim shorts, little tops and high heels to work in the hip hotel bar. After all, she was well aware that at least one of her colleagues took money to sleep with customers, and she had always been very careful not to give the wrong impression to the male clientele by being too flirtatious and she never ever gave out her phone number. In any case, for better or for worse, she had no time for a boyfriend in her life. Her life was full to overflowing from the moment she got up at six until she fell into bed worn out soon after midnight.

She checked into work punctually that evening, having earned several admonitions for being late when Claire failed to come home on time to take over charge of the children. Stashing her bag in the locker provided, she put on the shorts and the high heels that she had mercifully finally worn in and walked into the elegant black and white bar, with its eye-catching lighting and mirrored ceiling, to begin serving drinks. The black and white theme and the wonderfully opulent décor ran right through the boutique hotel, where no expense had been spared and where every comfort was on offer to those who could afford the high prices.

'Mr da Rocha is out on the terrace,' Roger, the bar manager, informed her.

'Who the heck is Mr da Rocha?' she asked.

'That guy you don't like. He's back,' Roger told her wryly and he lowered his head to whisper tautly, 'A fairly reliable source tells me that Mr da Rocha *bought* this place a couple of months ago, so I would watch my step if I were you because if he decides he wants you out, you'll be history.'

Freddie was drop-dead stunned by that piece of information and she stared wide-eyed after Roger as he moved off to attend to a customer at the bar.

Zac *owned* the hotel? How was it possible that a foul-mouthed, tattooed guy in ripped jeans and biker boots had *bought* a hotel in one of the most exclusive areas of London? She clenched her teeth in thwarted disbelief. Yes, Zac was a huge mystery because, no matter what he wore or how carelessly he spoke, he emanated a force field of power and arrogance and contrived to appear totally at home in a very up-market hotel. Practising her brightest smile, Freddie marched out to the terrace, which was unnervingly empty but for him.

And like a juggernaut parked in a too small parking space, Zac overfilled it, his devastating effect all the stronger because it had been so many weeks since she last saw him. He was wearing all black, which was a change from his usual denim blue jeans. Black jeans, black shirt, leather cuff on one arm, his St Jude necklace gleaming gold at his bronzed throat. Patron saint of lost causes, very appropriate, she thought inanely. But he was so outrageously gorgeous standing there that her mouth ran dry and her nipples tightened and her entire body leapt in a response that maddened her because it happened every time she saw him, like an alarm clock shrilling in her ear, reminding her that she was as weak and hormonal around him as every other young woman she saw staring at him with longing. While she might not stare, she was, at heart, no different from the rest of her sex, and the reminder rankled like a stone in her shoe she couldn't shake loose.

Lounging back against the boundary wall, Zac straightened the instant Freddie appeared, so tiny, so dainty she reminded him of a delicate doll. A doll he wanted to flatten down and spread on the nearest horizontal surface, he reminded himself, looking boldly into eyes that ranged from the colour of melted caramel to that of liquid chocolate. A wall would do perfectly well, he thought absently, so aroused at the sight of her he was threatening the fly in his new jeans, and the infuriating thing was that he didn't know exactly what it was about her that so turned him on every time she was within view.

'Mr…er da Rocha,' she pronounced, startling him with both the name and the undeniably false smile she had pasted on her lips because, most pointedly, she was careful never ever to smile at him.

And he knew right then that somebody had been talking and that she was somehow aware that he was not merely a hotel guest at The Palm Tree. Exasperation shimmered through him. He had bought the hotel for convenience, not for any form of recognition.

'I have a proposition for you,' Zac murmured huskily.

He had the most lethal electric sensuality Freddie had ever heard in a man's voice. He could make a drinks order sound like a caress that skimmed spectral fingers down her rigid spine.

'I think I've already heard that one, *sir*,' she tacked on tightly. 'And I'm going to pass on it—'

'No, you haven't heard this one,' Zac cut in with a raw impatience he did not even attempt to hide. 'I will give you a thousand pounds to spend an hour with me. And no, not in bed if that's what you're thinking. An hour *anywhere* in *any* place of your choosing.'

Her lashes fluttered up on utterly bewildered eyes. 'But why *would* you offer—?'

'I want to get to know you,' Zac lied. 'A conversation is all I'm asking for, nothing else. So, are you up for it or not?'

'Anywhere, any place?' she double-checked, because she didn't credit his desire to get to know her for a second.

'Anywhere, any place,' Zac confirmed.

Freddie straightened her stiff shoulders and thought fast. If he was fool enough to pay, she was bright enough to take advantage. 'Give me your phone number and I'll think about it,' she told him jerkily, barely able to credit that she was willing to sell her scruples down the river to spend even five minutes with him, never mind an hour!

'There would have to be no crude language and no touching,' she warned him carefully.

'I can handle that.' Zac gave her a huge charismatic smile that flashed white teeth and sent her heartbeat racing.

It was a crying shame that a man with his looks and presence should be so cynical and rough round the edges, Freddie reflected as he strode off the terrace, visibly satisfied with the result of his barefaced bribery. Of course, he didn't want to get to *know* her. He wanted to get into her underwear in the most basic way possible and her negative response had simply forced him to raise his game.

But how could she possibly turn down a thousand pounds with Eloise and Jack to consider? With that kind of money she could take them on a little holiday or finally establish a rainy-day fund for emergencies. Yes, she was being greedy and shameless to accept such an arrangement but, as long as he knew upfront that no sex would be involved, he only had himself to blame for his extravagance and his *huge* ego. And she knew that she was going to enjoy punishing him thoroughly for both flaws.

CHAPTER TWO

'ARE YOU WORRIED about something?' Freddie asked Claire gently, striving to redirect her anxiety about meeting up with Zac in an hour's time towards something hopefully less threatening to her peace of mind. 'You've seemed so preoccupied lately...'

Her aunt, a brunette with her hair tied up in a casual ponytail, shrugged a shoulder and almost squirmed in her seat beneath Freddie's troubled appraisal. 'Oh, you know...things get on top of me sometimes.'

'You must miss Richard,' Freddie said sympathetically, because Claire's boyfriend had recently gone out to Spain to help his parents set up the business they had bought out there. At the same time he was expected home within days.

'Obviously,' Claire muttered rather cuttingly, rising from the kitchen table with heightened colour in her cheeks. 'I've got some emails to catch up on. See you later.'

And there it was, the refusal to spill the beans

again, Freddie reflected ruefully while wondering if she should simply mind her own business because the two women had never been best friends who shared everything. Furthermore, didn't she have enough to worry about?

Ever since she had made that agreement with Zac da Rocha, she had been regretting it. Her worst sin was impulsiveness. What if the guy turned nasty? From his point of view, she would be wasting his time and he would probably refuse to cough up the money he had offered, so all she was likely to do was embarrass herself and infuriate him. Was that wise when he could—possibly—be her employer? Ridiculous as it still seemed to Freddie, the rumour of his ownership of the hotel was spreading in spite of the fact that for some strange reason he apparently didn't want anyone to know.

Regret and uncertainty stabbing at her nerves, she had tried to take a rain check on the arrangement she had made with him by text, but Zac was set on denying her any wriggle room while adding that he was looking forward to seeing her, which, in the circumstances, only made Freddie feel worse because by no stretch of the imagination was it going to be a date.

Yet, for all that awareness, Freddie found herself taking more care with her appearance than she usually did on such trips. Her hair was freshly washed and she put on her best jeans and newest top while also ensuring that the children looked presentable. Eloise danced alongside the buggy containing Jack because she adored the park where she could swing and run about. Freddie approached the bench by the central fountain where she had arranged to meet Zac and breathed in deep and slow.

'Who we meeting?' Eloise demanded again.

'A man. A…a friend,' Freddie fibbed.

'Name?' Eloise pressed.

'It's Zac,' Freddie told her reluctantly, fairly sure that Zac would not last five minutes in their company once he registered that she had called his bluff in the most basic way possible. Did he even have a sense of humour?

Freddie stood up to pace the instant she saw Zac in the distance. He was so tall he was easy to spot. Jack grizzled to get out of the buggy and, with a sigh, she freed him, praying that she could keep him out of the water because she had not brought spare clothing out with her. Jack had confounded all expectations by getting up and walking at ten months old on his sturdy little legs. He had never crawled, he had just pulled himself up to walk and Freddie had discovered that her baby boy was suddenly a toddler with even less wit than the average toddler because he was still so young.

Eloise pushed the empty buggy along the path, Jack at her side. Freddie focussed on Zac's approach, her heart beating very, very fast until it reached such a pitch that even breathing became a challenge. It was nerves, she told herself. He strode with the innate fluidity of a predator and she was hyperaware of every facet of him: the blue-black hair blowing back from his bronzed and perfect features, the sheer beauty of his bold masculinity in the sunlight, those strikingly light eyes of his, the colour of which she was still unsure of, glittering with the same charisma as his wide slashing smile. Oh, heavens, he was going to *hate* her, she thought with a sudden sharp pang of regret that startled her.

Were those kids with her? Surely not, Zac reasoned, deeming her too young for such a role while glancing around hopefully for another adult and failing to see one in the vicinity. They were her kids? *She* had kids? And not just a modest single one, but *two*? *Inferno*, what had he got himself into? But Zac had always been a quick study and light on his feet and he was careful not to betray an ounce of his discomfiture while feasting his attention on the slender blonde by the fountain. It was her body, he told himself urgently, just something about those seemingly fragile little bones and tiny curves that hugely turned him on. Or maybe it was the hair, thick and streaky blonde and definitely natural in his opinion, long twirling strands with a slight wave shifting in the breeze. Or was it the face, the unexpectedly dark eyes that were so much more unusual with that hair colour than blue? Or that incredibly voluptuous pink mouth of hers that left him painfully turned on?

Meu Deus, she was finally smiling at him and it lit up her solemn little face like the sun. True, the smile was a tad awkward and stiff, which it ought to be, considering that she had set him up with two kids in tow. Involuntarily, Zac was amused for no woman had ever tried to block him with children before, and he also knew that if he had known in advance what her reservations related to he would have run a mile, because kids and the freedom he valued so highly didn't work together at all. And how the hell could she even *try* to fulfil the bet with Vitale for him with two little kids around? To his intense annoyance, the possibility of retaining his precious sports car seemed to move further out of his grasp.

'Well, you said you wanted to get to know me,' Freddie reminded him with more than a little desperation, for the silence had stretched far longer than she could be comfortable with. 'And *this* is my life pretty much…the kids.'

Zac watched her settle down on the bench while the little girl hovered with huge dark eyes below her mop of blonde curls and the baby clung to her knees. 'What do you call them?' he asked.

'I'm Eloise,' the little girl informed him importantly while lifting up her dress to show off her underwear.

'Eloise, leave your dress alone,' Freddie inter-posed.

'And you're Auntie Freddie's friend, Zac,' Eloise completed, skipping over to him to grab his bare arm where a tattoo of a dragon writhed. 'What's that?'

'A dragon.'

'Like in my storybook?' Eloise screamed with excitement.

'And this is Jack,' Freddie supplied, her face pink with embarrassment.

'*Auntie* Freddie?' Zac queried, his hopes rising afresh while the little girl clambered uninvited onto his lap, the better to examine his tattoo.

'Get down, Eloise,' Freddie instructed.

Eloise ignored her. Zac lifted the child down onto the bench between them and extended his arm in the slender hope of getting some peace.

'I can't really talk about it here with little ears,' Freddie admitted awkwardly, wondering if ever a woman had been more punished for trying to out-face a man. 'But my sister...er...passed last year.'

'And there's no one else?' Zac pressed, insanely conscious of the little girl's eyes clinging to his.

'Well, there's my aunt, Claire, who's twenty-eight and their official foster carer, but my agreement with her is that she's the official but I do the caring,' Fred-die volunteered in a horrid rush that mortified her because she felt as if she were apologising for her unavailability. 'As you know I work evenings, so there's really no room in my life for anything else.'

'I'm not still trying to…gave up on that,' Zac lied.

He had so many tells when he lied, Freddie recognised, noting the downward shift of his outrageously long black lashes, the evasive gaze, the clenching of one hand on a long, powerful thigh. Yes, he was still interested in her but currently pretending not to be for some strange reason.

'So, why did you want to meet up, then?' she enquired, striving not to sound sarcastic because he had taken the presence of the kids like a gentleman, even if she was convinced that he was far from being one.

Jack wobbled over to him like a homing pigeon and clutched at both his knees, beaming up at Zac with a sunny Jack smile of acceptance. Zac unfroze and stood up with care, trying not to dislodge Jack. 'Let's walk,' he suggested. 'It'll occupy the children.'

It was well timed, with both her niece and nephew treating him like a wonderful and mesmerising new toy. When she had made the decision to meet Zac in the park with the children, it should have occurred to her that Eloise and Jack would be fascinated with him because they very rarely had any contact with men. Claire had complained bitterly about the way they hogged her boyfriend's attention when he came round.

'We'll move on to the playground,' she agreed, lifting Jack, who wailed in protest and putting him back into the buggy.

Finding himself in possession of a trusting little girl's hand, Zac strode along the path below the trees, trying and failing to slow his stride to match Eloise's tiny steps. Without further ado, he began telling Freddie about his bet with his brother, Vitale.

'My goodness, that's so childish…what age are you?' Freddie asked in sincere wonderment.

'Twenty-eight.'

'Really?' Her wondering gaze grew even wider. 'Maybe it's a boy thing, but I just can't imagine making such a crazy bet and risking losing something I valued out of pride.'

His nostrils flaring, Zac computed that far from complimentary comment and drew in a long steadying breath before continuing, 'Vitale was the guy I was with the day you had your…episode,' he selected finally, shooting her a sidewise glance.

'Oh, you mean when I screamed and shouted at you?' Freddie translated with unexpected amusement. 'Yeah, it was a rough day after too many rough days in a row…sorry about that. So, your brother was the nice guy?'

Zac jerked his chin in affirmation even while his temper rocketed at that unjust designation being bestowed on Vitale. What was so bloody nice about Vitale? His half-brother had hushed her like a sympathetic audience and every word he had spoken had been fake as hell! Hadn't she realised that? Was she blind or deaf? He wasn't fake or a smoothie like Vitale! But were those qualities what she found attractive in a man?

'And *the nice guy* who was present when you broke down,' Zac enunciated with raw precision, 'bet me that I couldn't bring you "all lovelorn and clingy", as he put it, to his precious royal ball at the end of this month.'

As Eloise released Zac's hand to race off ahead of them to the swings, Freddie stopped dead with the buggy, her face a mask of shock. *'Me?'*

'And suitably polished up to royal standards,' Zac said with even greater scorn.

'I don't do lovelorn and clingy,' Freddie muttered blankly, still struggling simply to accept that Zac could have a brother with some sort of *royal* connection. 'Are the two of you crazy competitors or something?'

'Or something,' Zac fielded non-committally. 'But I'm here today because I was wondering if, for a very generous *price*—'

'No,' Freddie slotted in flatly straight away. 'And don't embarrass me by quoting figures! I was annoyed with you last week when you offered to pay me for an hour of my time and I wanted to teach you a lesson by landing you with me and the kids, but this paying me nonsense *has* to stop now.'

Zac frowned, level black brows pleating, his bewilderment patent. 'But why?'

And he didn't get it, he *really* didn't get that it was offensive to try and buy people like products, she registered in frustration. 'Because it's wrong.'

His eyes were a very light, almost crystalline blue in the sunshine, she marvelled as he stared down at her, her brain momentarily a complete blank. 'You accept my tips,' he reminded her stubbornly.

'Because the tips go into a communal pot for *all* the staff and when I turned your tip down the first time, it naturally annoyed the other wait staff,' Freddie explained. 'That's why I returned and accepted it and didn't refuse again.'

Zac was furious at the explanation and immediately resolved to change the rules in the bar, so that Freddie got to keep her own tips: her sneakers were faded and had a hole in one toe. Even the buggy was threadbare—in fact all three of them looked poverty-stricken in comparison to the children he saw around the hotel. Jack lurched out of the buggy again and headed straight for his knees and Zac let him cling, grudgingly impressed by the baby's huge smile. Jack definitely knew how to make friends. Zac's wide, full mouth compressed.

'Obviously… I mean, I assume,' Freddie stumbled, unable to read the sleek, taut lines of Zac's darkly handsome face and trying not to offend, 'you're not short of money but people who *are* short of money have pride too.'

'But if I've got it and you need it, it's a simple exchange and not offensive,' Zac incised with ringing, argumentative conviction.

'I won't take that thousand pounds under any circumstances because it is wrong and it would make me feel like a con artist! Or like a person you could buy, like a hooker or something!' Freddie declared vehemently.

Passion fired her eyes to glowing gold, Zac noted absently, the fit of his jeans tightening as a wave of desire washed over his body. 'But that's not how I think of you,' he objected in a driven tone, wondering why absolutely everything had to be so infuriatingly complicated with her and hating it. He was reminded of Vitale and all *his* many dos and don'ts, which prevented his half-brother from enjoying the freedom that Zac cherished.

'How could you feel like a hooker when I haven't even touched you?' Zac asked thickly, thinking about touching her to such an extent that even a vacant swing was pushing him into highly inappropriate fantasies.

Freddie's heart was hammering again. Those eyes of his filled her vision, full of glitter and a kind of wild rebellion that was strangely appealing to a young woman who always, *always* played safe. She so badly wanted him to understand her point of view that she wanted to shake him into properly listening, which she knew he wasn't doing.

'*Eu quero voce…* I want you,' Zac growled in English the instant he realised what he had spoken in his own language. '*Why* is that wrong?'

'I didn't say it was wrong!' Freddie gasped. 'I said it was wrong to try and use money to tempt me.'

Zac was on firmer ground now and he extended a hand to wind long brown fingers very slowly through the fall of her hair, his every hunting instinct on high alert in an adrenalin charge beyond anything he had ever experienced. 'But you already want me,' he contended with devastating assurance. 'You wanted me the first time you saw me, so why are we still arguing about it?'

And Freddie deflated as suddenly as a balloon that had had an unfortunate collision with a pin. Colour surged hotly up her face in a crimson tide. That *he* should know that with such appalling certainty, that he should feel in his bones what she had studiously denied even to herself, shook her rigid and utterly silenced her.

Zac tugged her closer and bent his arrogant dark head lower and lower until he finally found her mouth, where the sultry sweet taste of her released a surge of such powerful lust he trembled with it. He eased her up into his arms, ignoring Jack's pleas to be lifted, indeed forgetting the child's very existence.

Freddie had never ever had a kiss of that magnitude. Admittedly, life had ensured that she had not had the opportunity to have many kisses, but when she got her arms wrapped round Zac's neck for the merest fraction of a second she felt as if she never ever wanted to let go because she felt safe, safe for the first time since she had lost her parents, safe as if nothing bad could ever happen to her again. And that unholy kiss, the passionate pressure of that wide, sensual mouth on hers, the plunge of his tongue, that tiny provocative flick he performed across the roof of her mouth… All of a sudden, Freddie wanted what she had never wanted before and she wanted it so very badly, an ache stirred between her slender thighs, heat bursting in her pelvis, her nipples tightening so hard and fast it prickled and *hurt*.

Zac set her down on the ground again, vindicated in his every claim, rejoicing in her responsiveness, wishing he had had the chance to demonstrate their potential chemistry when he had first met her. Showing worked better for him than telling, he acknowledged, now in a good enough mood to scoop up a red-faced, crying Jack and hold him against his shoulder to console him for being ignored.

Freddie almost fell over when Zac returned her to earth. She was dizzy, disorientated, her brain refusing to function, her legs wobbling while her mouth felt swollen and hot. Her hands clenched into fists because she wanted to hit Zac for that lethal demonstration of power over her. Her pride was stung, her heart was still racing and for one unforgivable instant she had forgotten the children. Eloise was shouting to be pushed on the swing and Jack? Jack, astonishingly, she registered, was in Zac's arms, his little head laid down trustingly on Zac's shoulder as the need for his morning nap overcame his little body. Since Freddie could not think of a single thing to say, she rushed over to push her niece on the swing, leaving Zac standing.

Zac scanned her stiff and flushed little face with growing annoyance. What was wrong with her now? *This* was why he didn't date, didn't chase women, didn't ever make an effort. He thought about planting Jack back in the buggy and strapping him in and leaving, but Jack was clutching his jacket in one hand and emanating a rather endearing little snore of contentment, a contentment that would be shattered by any sudden movement. It would be good practice for him when he became a father some day, he told himself begrudgingly. His own child might be horrible; at least Jack was smiley with relatively simple needs.

Eloise, though, would be more demanding, he recognised as the little girl called for him to push her instead of her aunt and he studiously ignored the invite. And then the oddest memory occurred to him, a very early one as he cried for his mother's attention and failed to receive it. Before he knew what he was doing, Zac had stalked over to the swings, passed Jack over to Freddie, who was still acting like a frozen popsicle, and he had taken over pushing the swing. Sometimes children *should* get what they wanted, he decided generously. Just because *he* hadn't didn't mean others should be disappointed too.

Freddie defrosted while Zac pushed Eloise because he was being so unexpectedly helpful and it was very immature to want to punish him for making her enjoy a kiss. What was a kiss? Or what was it about a single kiss that made her dangerously crave another? It was too risky for someone in her position, she reasoned unhappily.

'I can't have a fling with you!' she whispered to Zac over the top of her niece's head.

'What's a "fling"?' Zac fielded in his usual speaking voice.

'Work it out!' Freddie urged impatiently.

'But why not?' he asked equally baldly. 'You're not married. You don't have a boyfriend.'

'We can't talk about it here,' Freddie incised, her colour rising again.

'And whose fault is that? *You* arranged this,' Zac reminded her harshly.

'You were *supposed* to walk away and lose interest!' Freddie flung at him accusingly, striving not to focus on that tantalisingly tempting mouth of his.

'I'm obstinate,' Zac declared with a sudden slashing grin of one-upmanship that emanated extraordinary charisma. 'It takes more energy to put one over me, *meu pequenino.*'

Freddie dropped her head, dark streaky golden hair semi-screening her troubled expression, because she abruptly recognised that on some level she was dragging out their meeting for her own purposes and there was no point in wasting Zac's time when she had no plans to let anything go any further. 'Look, it's time for us to go,' she declared, fighting her awareness of his compelling appeal with all her might.

'Or I could treat you to lunch.'

'No, Jack will scream if he's wakened,' Freddie muttered woodenly, wondering how Zac had contrived to travel from hateful to almost bearable in the course of an hour and hurriedly squashing the pointless reflection. 'We have to go home.'

Zac shrugged a wide shoulder and fell into step beside her as she gathered up Eloise and lowered Jack back into the buggy. 'Aren't you leaving?' Freddie demanded in surprise.

'I'll see you home,' Zac countered stiffly, angrily aware that his welcome seemed to have worn out, questioning why he should care when there were so many more available women around.

Freddie didn't know how to shake him off politely and she felt she had to be polite because, whether she liked it or not, he had been a good sport and at least he was no longer trying to stuff banknotes in her direction.

'You must have *some* social life,' Zac remarked drily, walking down the small dismal street of terraced houses.

'Not really,' Freddie mumbled, fumbling for her key and about to unlock the door when it opened without warning and framed Claire. 'Oh, hi, Claire!' she began.

'And who's this?'

Zac extended a hand and introduced himself and Claire invited him in, completely ignoring Freddie's frantic mute grimaces from behind him.

'Hot, hot, *hot*,' Claire whispered in surprising delight as Freddie passed by her into the cramped hall and Zac lifted in the buggy. 'I'll put on the kettle, shall I?' she added with enthusiasm.

Freddie took Jack upstairs to his cot and when she went down to the lounge, Zac was drinking coffee, comfortably ensconced like a welcome guest while Claire acted as hostess. Maybe he would be attracted to Claire, she thought abruptly and then killed the suspicion, taken aback by how something visceral inside her rose in rage at that idea.

'I'll babysit for you so that you can go out with Zac,' Claire announced, startling her with that unprecedented offer. 'I keep on telling Freddie that she *has* to make her own life beyond the kids. You're not working tonight, are you?'

'Well, no, but—'

'Thanks, Claire. I'll pick you up at eight,' Zac delivered, sidestepping Eloise's offer of her dragon storybook and vaulting upright to seize the moment.

Freddie chased him into the hall but he was too quick for her, already out of the front door and down the steps before she could reach him.

'Why did you do that?' she returned to ask Claire. 'I don't want to go out with him.'

'Of course, you do. He's gorgeous,' Claire parried crushingly. 'All work and no play will make Freddie a very dull girl and if I can help you to see that I'll be happier.'

Silenced by that assurance, reluctant to get into a disagreement with Claire, whose opinions tended to be strident, Freddie swallowed hard. She didn't want to spend more time with Zac when she found him so attractive and was finally admitting that to herself. But pursuing that attraction in any way would be futile. She didn't want a sleazy one-night stand with him and that was all he was after, a little recreational sex to fill a fleeting moment. That wasn't her, would never be her. After a frightening attack in her teens, her sister had gone on to have a lot of casual sex and that was ultimately how she'd ended up with her creepy boyfriend. Freddie was still a virgin because she had had little time for a social life, but she still knew that she wouldn't settle for a meaningless fling. She wanted feelings involved as well as mutual respect and consideration and Zac wasn't programmed to offer any of that. She needed more before she could give her trust and if that was old-fashioned, well, she was content to be old-fashioned.

Zac was equally discomfited at the prospect of the evening ahead. He had never been on a date, had never sought that kind of relationship and hadn't a clue how to go about it. But he had no problem in asking his other brother, Angel, for clarification when he met him out of his office for coffee that afternoon, because his Greek sibling didn't annoy him the way Vitale did. Angel had a much more laid-back and less judgemental attitude.

'Never?' Angel queried in some surprise. 'By the sound of it, your sex life is pretty basic.'

'Very basic,' Zac admitted without embarrassment. 'But I really want this woman.'

'Merry would probably be more help than me,' Angel acknowledged wryly, referring to his new wife. 'I screwed up very badly with her, so we never really dated as such. Take your lady for a drink or dinner, keep it casual.'

Zac's ego was mollified by Angel's confession, but he need not have worried because Freddie had agonised throughout the afternoon before finally texting him her suggestion that they try go-karting.

Zac was astonished by the suggestion because

it seemed ridiculously boyish and competitive for a woman who struck him as ultra-feminine, but it appealed much more to his energetic nature than an evening that had to be based on conversation. It did not once occur to him that he was being managed.

Freddie was delighted by Zac's assent. The setting would ensure she wasn't silly and prevent him from getting too handsy. When Claire looked at her in almost comical surprise when she told her where they were going, Freddie simply laughed.

Zac arrived to pick her up on a motorbike, a big black and gold beast that disconcerted her when she had expected him to arrive in some flash sports car. He got off the bike and said very drily, as if he was offering her a huge compliment, 'I've never had a girl on the back of my bike before.'

'First time for everything,' Freddie quipped, putting on the helmet he handed her. 'I haven't been on a motorbike before.'

He flipped out the foot pegs for her, climbed back astride and voiced several terse instructions. With difficulty, Freddie hopped up behind him and wrapped her arms round him, belatedly appreciating that, while a car would have marooned them in dangerous privacy, a bike offered physical intimacy of a possibly more dangerous kind. Her palms rested against rock-hard abs, her fingers brushing against his belt, and then the bike started up and vibrations travelled through her from head to foot in an unexpectedly exciting way.

She rested her face against the back of his jacket, strands of his black hair whipping against her brow, and the scent of him engulfed her like a rip tide, sent to torment. He smelled clean and male with a hint of some exotic cologne and the combination was one to savour, she acknowledged absently, marvelling that such a reality could make her skin tingle and her body heat while she felt every flex of his powerful abdominal muscles shift beneath her clinging hands. Her fingers spread against the heat of him, her own body savouring the connection in the most astonishing way.

Zac wanted to push her hands down to where he really needed her attention below the belt where she was being so very careful not to touch him. Why was she so inhibited? What did she have against pleasure? He had to work that out before sheer sexual frustration drove him crazy. It had been weeks since he had had a woman and that was a new development for him and not one he appreciated. After all, sex was one of life's greatest free pleasures and a need he was accustomed to indulging in regularly.

Why was a single woman as attracted to him as he was to her refusing him? Something in her past? What else could it be? Had she been assaulted? *Abused?* His guts twisted at the suspicion because he despised men who used physical force against the weaker and more vulnerable. *Meu Deus*, could she be even more complicated than he had already recognised? Once again he asked himself angrily, *Why her?* Why was he chasing a woman for the first time in his life? Why wasn't he simply moving on? He swore furiously to himself then that if she refused him again, he would forget about her and seek his pleasure elsewhere…

CHAPTER THREE

As HE PEELED off the last of his protective gear, Zac glanced across at Freddie and his wide, sensual mouth quirked with concealed amusement. There she was, benched after being red-flagged for a safety violation, her face still a mask of angry mortification. Yet she had initially gone onto the track with all the risk-taking verve of a nervous elderly lady and then Zac had flashed past her, a manoeuvre that had evidently unleashed her competitive instincts, and the die had been cast as she raced into pursuit of him in flagrant disregard of her apparent lack of experience on the track.

'Go on...*laugh*,' she urged sulkily, her annoyed gaze challenging him to do his worst while even then noticing the natural animal rhythm of his fluid stride. He walked lightly for so large a man yet testosterone seeped from his very pores. Even in a crowded location, his stunning looks stood out and guaranteed female turned heads and interested stares. Her stiff cheekbones flushed on the sinking acknowledgement that she was woman enough to be proud of being seen with him.

'When you suggested it, I assumed go-karting was a favourite pastime of yours.'

'You must be kidding. I've only been once and that was years ago…a birthday treat with the foster family we were staying with then.'

Zac took her breath away by simply lifting her off her feet and settling her down on the back of his bike. 'Foster family? *We?*' he queried with a frown.

'Never mind,' Freddie parried, seeing no reason to share her past with him when he was about to take her home.

Resting her cheek against his broad back as the bike glided through the traffic, Freddie closed her eyes, the oddest sensation of regret tugging infuriatingly at her while her body reacted with heat and awareness to the physical contact with his. The date, as such, was done and dusted and he had to now recognise that she was scarcely the sexy temptress of his dreams. He had enjoyed himself though, for Zac and speed were a perfect match, so hopefully there would be no hard feelings and her job would be safe because she really could not afford to lose her job, she thought fearfully.

Lifting her off the bike, Zac unclipped her helmet. As he herded her forward, he tossed his key fob to the doorman and addressed him in a foreign language. 'Where the heck are we?' Freddie demanded, cursing herself for having drifted off into her thoughts and failing to pay attention.

And even by the time she bleated that foolish question she knew exactly where she was and she cringed because she had never walked through the front entrance of The Palm Tree before. Staff had a side entrance and the bar was separate as well and employees were instructed to stay in their designated zone. Ahead of her and below the magnificent crystal chandeliers stretched a blur of mirrored reception counter that was dazzling and disorientating in the bright light.

Something remarkably like panic grabbed Freddie. 'I can't be in here... I *work* here!' she exclaimed in dismay, trying to pull away from Zac's controlling hand at her hip.

Zac grabbed her up into his arms as though she were Eloise and strode into his private lift before setting her down.

'Let me go, for goodness' sake!' Freddie launched at him furiously as he slid her down his long, lean body, ensuring that she missed out on not a single angle of his lean, muscular physique. 'I'm not coming up to your penthouse with you!'

'Yes, you are,' Zac countered without hesitation. 'I have food waiting for us.'

'I'm not hungry!' she protested contrarily.

'And I'm not an abuser of women and dislike being treated as though I am,' Zac replied very, *very* drily.

Colour ran in a hot tide up beneath Freddie's pale complexion and she collided with narrowed eyes the shade of crushed ice, glittering like a dangerous glacier in sunlight below a black lush fringe of lashes. 'That's not how I'm treating you.'

'It is,' he contradicted. 'And I don't like it. I would never touch you without your permission.'

A maddening need to apologise assailed Freddie and she fought it off, examining her behaviour, conceding that she might have come off a little hysterical in her rigid need to protect herself around a man. 'Look, I have to work here, and obviously I don't want to be seen inside *your* penthouse.'

'And maybe, just maybe,' Zac incised in a lethal undertone, those eyes luminous and cold as polar stars, 'I'm tired of doing everything *your* way, *meu pequenino.*'

Freddie compressed her lips and studied her scuffed trainers in the rushing silence. Her muscles ached with the tension in the air and her tummy performed a nauseous flip.

'When were you in foster care?' Zac continued smoothly as he thrust open the door of what she assumed to be the penthouse suite, because a superb wall of glass overlooked the twinkling lights of the city skyline that bounded one side of the huge room.

Freddie was busy looking around herself at a level of luxury way beyond her experience. There was a tiny elegant kitchen alcove in one corner, not one to be taken seriously, for few who could afford the rates for the penthouse would wish to cook for themselves in a hotel renowned for its cuisine. Another couple of doors led off the main area, which was furnished with a massive wall television and buttery soft leather sofas, currently strewn with car magazines.

'Freddie?' he prompted, amused by her frank curiosity about her surroundings.

Freddie relocated her wits, still careful not to look at him. 'My parents were killed in a car crash when I was ten. I had a completely happy childhood up until then, not so much after that,' she admitted stiffly, food scents tugging at her nostrils, provoking an embarrassingly loud and needy growl from her stomach.

Freddie spoke quickly, fearful that he had heard her tummy grumble. 'What about you? Where did you grow up?'

'A *fazenda*…a ranch in Brazil.' Zac lifted the cover on the food trolley with a flourish. 'Help yourself,' he urged.

Grateful to have something to do with her knotted hands, Freddie reached for a plate while scolding herself for her nerves. Being alone with a man was no big deal and it was time she got over her hang-ups from the years spent living with her sister. In any case, Lauren had been the victim of the abuse, not Freddie, who had merely been a powerless shrinking presence. Zac had probably done her a favour by calling her on her attitude to him. After all, some day in the future, she might want a man of her own and she wouldn't want to scare him off by acting weird, would she? Her spine stretching out of the stiffness she had maintained, she struggled to relax her defences.

'I would never have picked you out as a country boy,' Freddie confided as she ate the convenient mini finger foods she had piled on her plate, perched on the edge of a too comfortable sofa.

Zac's beautifully shaped mouth quirked. 'I'm not, although I'm quite interested in breeding pedigree horses,' he admitted, startling her afresh.

Zac watched her ease back into the sofa as though it were a potentially dangerous manoeuvre. Her feet left the floor and she crossed her legs like an elf, making herself at home with him for the first time, and he got a rush out of that display of relaxation, which unsettled him. It was only that she was prickly, difficult and an unknown quantity and he loved a challenge, he told himself squarely. Maybe without really noticing he had got bored with the constant sexual come-ons and the easy conquests. And Freddie was different, so very different from the sort of women he usually bedded. She also looked ridiculously cute sitting there, he acknowledged uneasily, frowning at that aberrant thought.

'I also wanted to ask if you've thought any more about joining me in that bet I mentioned this morning,' Zac delivered, getting back down to business with a strong sense of relief.

Her vivid little face screwed up tight and she studied him in surprise. 'You're *still* on about that?' she questioned.

Zac shrugged a broad shoulder. 'I don't give up on anything easily.'

No, if she could peel him apart Freddie was convinced she would find the word 'determined' stamped through him as though he were a stick of rock. She parted her lips to protest and then closed them again, wanting to be civil. 'I have the children to look after,' she said finally.

'And I could easily hire a nanny,' Zac traded, once again refusing to take no for an answer. 'We could have a lot of fun at Vitale's royal ball. I'm sure you'd enjoy getting all togged up in a fancy designer dress as much as any woman.'

'No, sorry,' Freddie muttered, crushing down the temptation offered by that treacherous word, 'fun'. For a split second, she considered the offer of a nanny's help and then suppressed the idea again because, with Claire's current mood, she did not want to risk rocking the boat. It was out of the question. Certainly not while Claire was currently saddled with a boyfriend flying out to Spain whenever he could to help his parents set up their new business. It would be the worst possible time for Freddie to start demonstrating a desire to fly free on her own behalf.

Zac sank down beside her on the sofa, suddenly way too close for comfort, she told herself anxiously. Or was that prickling fullness in her breasts and the sudden tiny betraying burst of heat between her thighs a mortifying wish for him to get closer still? Colour bled up beneath her skin, heating her all over.

'But that's crazy,' Zac argued.

'You don't know when to quit, do you?' Freddie remarked in reproach. 'I don't want to talk about this.'

'But I do,' Zac parried with irrepressible enthusiasm, light eyes shimmering like stars in the dusk light. 'I'd like to spend more time with you and I can't understand why you would fight that when you want it too.'

Eloise and Jack, Freddie reflected without speaking. 'I *don't* want to spend more time with you, though,' she told him drily, running for her only possible escape hatch.

'Why do you lie about it?' Zac demanded with sudden lancing impatience.

Freddie breathed in deep. 'I'm not lying,' she told him, looking back at him steadily, literally *willing* him to believe what she was saying.

His big hands came up to cup her cheekbones, long controlling fingers sliding into her hair to fasten to her skull, and she couldn't move an inch, brown eyes dilating with an enervating mixture of excitement and dismay.

'Liar,' he growled again.

'Just because I won't say what you want to hear doesn't mean I'm lying!' Freddie proclaimed in desperation.

The silence between them smouldered as if someone had set it on fire, brown eyes clashing with volatile light grey condemnation, and then he took her mouth with a wild, seething passion unlike anything she had ever felt before. It was like being swept away by a tidal wave, like sticking a finger in an electric socket or hitching a ride on a rocket because one minute she was grounded, the next she was flying high on a hunger that consumed her with its ferocious urgency. Sensation roared through her trembling body with every delving exploration of his tongue. He lowered a hand to crush the slight pout of her aching breast and she almost spontaneously combusted inside the prison of her flesh, her body screaming for more while she kissed him back with both hands laced tightly into the luxuriant depths of his long black hair.

In a sudden movement, Zac tore himself free, breathing heavily and raking a hand roughly through his tousled hair as he sprang upright again. 'So, *why* do you lie about how I make you feel? What's your game?' he demanded rawly.

'G-Game?' she stammered blankly, focusing on the prominent bulge at his denim-clad groin, and then on the stray black hairs still caught between her greedily clutching fingertips.

'Your agenda, because obviously there *is* one,' Zac bit out. 'Evidently it's not money.'

'No, it's not,' she agreed, stricken, hastily unfolding her legs and sliding upright on knees that wobbled because sheer shock was still rocking her. Shock that *he* could make her feel like that and that he should be the one with sufficient control to back off, *not* her, as it should have been in all fairness, she acknowledged guiltily. 'I don't have an agenda, Zac.'

Zac shot her a chillingly angry appraisal. 'Oh, I think you do. I think you're one of those archaic women who thinks the longer she says no, the keener I'll become!' he spelt out with derision, thinking of how she had become rather more encouraging since she had learned that he owned the hotel that employed her. 'That doesn't work for me. I don't do keen with women.'

'I didn't think you did,' Freddie told him, lifting her chin in a defiant signal of intent that Zac was unaccustomed to receiving from a woman. 'I've known from the start that all you want is a one-night stand and I certainly wouldn't waste my time or yours playing games with you. I don't want or need a man in my life right now but I don't mind admitting… just so you can see how *very* unsuited we are…that I would want more caring and commitment than a one-night stand. So, anyway, thanks for the evening out and the food.'

And with that, Freddie sidestepped him and stalked out of the door in high dudgeon.

Her eyes were stinging with tears and she furiously dashed them away in the lift. He had only confirmed what she had already guessed about the level of his interest and it was at rock-bottom level: sex. Talking about caring and commitment to a guy like that was undignified and humiliating, she censured herself angrily. Why had she bothered saying those stupid things? You couldn't ask or magically wish into being what wasn't being offered and Zac wasn't chasing a waitress for anything more lasting than a spirited toss between the sheets. Of course, there was also his crazy wager, which his stupid brother had involved her in by choosing her as the target of a bad joke. The royal brother had seen her hostility towards Zac and had known it would be a very tall order for Zac to bring her to the ball acting 'lovelorn'. Lovelorn, what a very outdated word, she thought wearily as she climbed on a bus home, planning the little white lie she would give Claire and certainly not the unlovely truth that she wasn't prepared to be quite as much fun as other young women her age.

Should she have considered a one-night stand? No, no, where was her brain travelling now? Yes, she had been very attracted to him but not enough to ditch long-held convictions. She would have felt used and foolish if she had slept with him; she also would have wanted more from him than he was prepared to give and that would have hurt her. And she might already be feeling hurt, but she rather suspected she would have felt even worse had she become intimate with Zac and then had to serve drinks to his next casual lover. It was better to play safe, she reasoned, wiser to stand by her beliefs and stay on an even keel.

When she got home, Claire was out and a babysitter was installed. Just managing to pay the babysitter with what she had in her purse, she was too restless to slide into bed and go straight to sleep the way she always did. Instead she went browsing on her aunt's laptop, snooping online to satisfy the curiosity that Zac had aroused. That exercise piled shock on shock! The Quintal da Rocha diamond mines in Russia and South Africa *belonged* to Zac and his brother was a Crown Prince. She recalled the diamond studs in one of his ears and his charismatic confidence and slowly marvelled that she had simply not worked out for herself that Zac's striking level of blazing assurance was only innate in someone of wealth.

Yet she, biased as she was against men, had immediately assumed he was some sort of chancer up to no good when she'd first seen him, she conceded ruefully, condemning him on the slender facts that he was breathtakingly good-looking and bold because Lauren's vicious boyfriend, Cruz, had had rather similar characteristics. Annoyed by her misconceptions and even more annoyed by the unhappiness dogging her, she forced herself to go to bed. Her sole consolation was that Zac would surely soon be off on his travels again to attend his royal brother's ball. She had satisfied almost all her curiosity with a series of searches. But she also knew that she would find it easier to get back to normal if Zac left the hotel for a while…or stopped using the hotel bar.

When Freddie walked out on him, Zac punched the wall with so much force that blood dripped down it and then he swore in every language he knew even though he knew that on one level she was right and there was no way on earth they could meld their respective wants and wishes. Caring? Commitment? Zac very nearly shuddered with distaste at the concept. He didn't know how to do either and he had no desire to learn. As he was, he was free as a bird and he had no plans to change that pleasurable state, certainly not for a woman. Women were always available, tall, short, curvy, thin—he wasn't particular. At least he hadn't been until he had met *her*. He would get drunk and wash her out of his mind, he decided with grim determination.

What he could not understand was what he had found so attractive about her in the first place! Possibly a man reached a certain age and was programmed to crave a different kind of woman. Maybe it could even be his father's genes at play. Charles Russell was certainly a man who liked to settle down with women in committed relationships. He had freely admitted that he would have married Zac's mother if he had got the chance and was currently seriously spending time with Angel's very glam grandma-in-law, Sybil.

Zac shook his head in bewildered anger while arrogantly marvelling at Freddie's resistance to him. Then he found himself wondering abstractedly if anyone would ever take the time to read Eloise that dragon story and, with another curse word of finality, rolled his eyes heavenward and consigned the whole Freddie debacle to history and oblivion. He would attend the ball alone...so what? No big deal, was it? He *liked* being alone; he *preferred* his own company.

CHAPTER FOUR

ONLY TWO DAYS LATER, Freddie's whole world im-
ploded.

'I did warn you last year that I wouldn't *do* this for
ever,' Claire reminded the younger woman briskly,
having announced her imminent plans to move to
Spain with her boyfriend. 'I've already given social
services a month's notice, so they'll be looking for
a new foster home for Eloise and Jack…although
I got the impression they're actually hoping to put
them up for adoption now. Cruz finally acknowledged paternity and signed off any interest in them.
Oh, Freddie, for heaven's sake, *don't* look at me like
I'm a monster!'

Freddie was trembling and biting her lip hard,
determined not to vent any of the very emotional
feelings flying through her head and brimming on
her lips. 'I'm not. I'm shocked, that's all, but you
did warn me before we got the kids,' she conceded,
striving to be fair. 'It's just I thought our arrangement would last a bit longer—'

'And maybe it would've done if I hadn't met Richard,' Claire cut in with a grimace. 'I was in a bad place when I agreed to take on the kids with you but now my life's opening up again. Richard will be the chef in his parents' restaurant and I'll work front of house. We're getting the little apartment above the restaurant to live in…it's nothing fancy but it'll do us fine and it will be a fresh start for me.'

Freddie tried very hard not to be selfish and not to surrender to a heart that felt as if it were being torn apart inside her. When she had begun living with Claire, Claire had been getting over a broken engagement and she had been unemployed. Fostering the children had suited the brunette back then, giving her the breathing space she had needed to rethink her future, and then Richard had entered her life.

'Yes,' Freddie agreed, struggling to block out the upsetting images of Eloise's and Jack's distress at being parted from her, because they had never lived without her in their lives. It would be *her* job to try and prepare the children for the changes ahead, she warned herself sternly, *her* role to ensure that any move went as smoothly as possible.

Claire planted her hand firmly on the back of her niece's tautly spread fingers. 'They're not *our* kids, Freddie.'

'But they feel like it.' Tears were openly swimming in Freddie's eyes.

'To you, not to me, I'm afraid.' Claire sighed. 'They're Lauren's kids. She chose to have them.'

'I don't think she *chose* anything,' Freddie protested.

'She was an addict. She made her mistakes and I don't feel the need to make sacrifices in her memory and neither should *you*,' Claire emphasised stridently. 'Haven't you already given up enough for those kids? OK…grieve, but let them go and live your own life now.'

'That's the problem. I don't *want* to let them go!' Freddie sobbed helplessly. 'I love them like they're my own!'

'But they're not yours *or* mine,' Claire reminded her single-mindedly. 'I don't even know yet if I want to have children! Why aren't you thinking about how Lauren's lifestyle destroyed yours? You should've gone to university, should've let her go but instead you hung in there trying to save someone who refused to be saved.'

'I know… I know,' Freddie gasped in grudging acknowledgement and sniffed into the tissue she had grabbed, struggling to master her turbulent emotions, for Claire's reminder had roused deep sadness for the once loving sister she had lost. 'But I couldn't turn my back on Eloise.'

'You'll have to learn how to step back now,' the brunette pointed out with the coolness of her pragmatic temperament. 'Let them go, Freddie, and move on with your own life like I'm doing.'

* * *

The day he got back from Lerovia, Zac wasn't looking for Freddie but he inevitably noticed her the instant she came on shift, walking strangely slowly, seemingly drained of her usual energy. He lounged back fluidly in his chair on the terrace, reminding himself that he no longer had an interest there. He watched while she took an order from a table of drunken men, city types, sharply suited, arrogantly convinced of their right to torment the cute little waitress with catcalls and comments. She kept her head down, doing her job by rote, her delicate profile set.

But when she returned with the tray, the guy on the outside seat ran his hand up the back of her slender thigh, fingers sidling up under the hem of her shorts. Zac stiffened, long, powerful thighs bracing. She stepped back, saying something, and the hand fell back; however, as she served the rest of the drinks the guy simply grabbed her, dragging her down onto his lap by force. Zac exploded out of his seat like a volcano. He was well aware that uninvited physical contact plunged Freddie into panic mode.

Freddie froze, trying to stay calm, recognising that the guy who had grabbed her was simply showing off, potentially not meaning any actual harm. And then suddenly she was plucked off the guy and set aside and her assailant was airborne, being shaken by someone much larger as a terrier shook a rat. And the customer was not a small man, yet he was being held off his feet and controlled like a dangling puppet and there were fear and consternation in his red sweaty face, his brash smart comments dying an immediate death.

'Let him down,' Freddie told Zac in shock once she realised who had stepped in to rescue her.

But sheer outrage had flushed Zac's perfect features, his light eyes bright as a silver sword blade in the dimness of the bar, his rage at the man's behaviour unconcealed.

'The waitress is here to bring you drinks, nothing else,' Zac informed the offending customer in a raw controlled undertone. 'You don't get to touch. She's not for sale like the drinks.'

'Put him down,' Freddie urged again, shaken by Zac's wrathful intervention and embarrassed by all the attention now coming their way, not to mention the bar manager and the burly bouncer now approaching them, eager to avoid an incident.

'If that's what you want,' Zac drawled grudgingly, slowly lowering the guy to the ground again.

'It is. Thanks,' Freddie proffered uneasily, keen to dial the tone down because Zac had looked as if he wanted to do a lot more than hold the guy in the air. Zac had looked as though he wanted to punch him and was barely restraining the urge to do so.

Zac stared down at her, noticing that her eyes were swollen and red rimmed. 'Bring me an espresso,' he told her casually, 'and whatever you want for yourself, and then you'll join me for a break.'

'It's not time for me to have a break.'

'It is now,' Zac told her without skipping a beat, pulling out the I'm-the-boss card without an ounce of self-consciousness, his assurance absolute.

Freddie duly collected two coffees from the bar and walked out onto the terrace into the bright sunlight to carry her tray to Zac's corner table. He ranged back in his seat like a panther forced into a reluctant retreat, luxuriant black hair feathering round his breathtakingly handsome bronzed features, only accentuating silvery pale blue eyes laced with lancing enquiry.

'What's wrong with you?' he demanded of her, because she looked as though a light had gone off inside her.

'There's nothing wrong,' she told him evasively.

Zac widened his stunning ebony-lashed eyes in scornful disagreement. 'Do I look that stupid?' he traded drily. 'Sit down and tell me what's happened.'

Freddie settled down into the seat opposite, her limbs heavy and clumsy to do her bidding because sleepless nights extracted a cost. 'I'm losing the kids,' she admitted with gruff abruptness. 'It's…painful…'

'Eloise and Jack? How can you lose them?' Zac questioned with a frown.

And she explained in as few words as possible about Claire and Richard's plans and shared the insights gained from her own general enquiries with the social services earlier that same day. 'I haven't got enough to offer…to foster or adopt them,' she admitted in pained conclusion. 'I'm only twenty-two, without a reliable income or a settled home. I can't offer them a mother and a father, so I wouldn't be a serious contender if they're putting my niece and nephew up for adoption.'

Zac breathed in deep, fascinated by her sudden rush of candour. 'How long have you been with them?'

Freddie's triangular face tightened, soft mouth tightening. 'Since they were born. My sister, Lauren, was a heroin addict. She wasn't capable of looking after Eloise and I stayed with her because someone had to do it.'

Zac gazed into her melted caramel eyes and dropped his scrutiny, unhappily encountering the soft pert swell of her unconfined breasts stirring as she shifted back into her seat opposite him, the light fabric of her top outlining the delectable contours of her delicate curves. He wondered how much of a bastard he was to notice her sexual allure in the middle of such a conversation but the heavy readiness at his groin was inescapable. Desire thrummed hungrily through his big powerful frame and with a very male sense of relief he celebrated the return of his libido, which had proved unsettlingly absent and inactive while he was in Lerovia. He wanted Freddie and substitutes, he had discovered, wouldn't do, no matter how beautiful and alluring they were.

'The children are very attached to you,' he remarked uncomfortably, wondering why he had even encouraged such a conversation in the circumstances. 'But perhaps *two* parents *would* be better for them than one.'

In dismay and hurt at that statement, Freddie gazed back at Zac's lean, hard-boned face, involuntarily mesmerised by the glow of those glittering light eyes below lush black lashes, her body suddenly turned taut and growing uncomfortably hot in places she didn't want to acknowledge. Even without trying, Zac contrived to emanate a powerful wave of electrifying sexual magnetism.

'I had only one parent and she was mostly absent during my childhood,' Zac divulged unexpectedly. 'I loved her but she wasn't up to the challenge.'

'Oh…' Freddie muttered awkwardly.

'She had good intentions but she put my stepfather first and he didn't want her to have anything to do with me because I wasn't his child,' Zac admitted curtly, already questioning why he was making such a personal admission. 'Having another parent around would have been a big improvement for me while I was growing up.'

Well, that was telling her, Freddie conceded unhappily, wishing the dialogue had gone another way so that she wouldn't have to feel that her powerful need to hang onto her sister's children was an entirely selfish urge. Zac quite clearly *did* believe that, if there was a choice, two parents would invariably be preferable to one.

'When do you have to give them up?' Zac prompted quietly.

Freddie lost colour and gave him a speaking look of reproach, her eyes burning with tears. 'The end of the month, before Claire leaves the UK. They'll go into foster care initially, unless the authorities identify a potential adoptive couple beforehand,' she told him painfully. 'And perhaps they will because they're attractive children, young enough to become part of a new family. It's probably horribly selfish of me to want to keep them with me when I don't have much to offer in terms of material things.'

Zac studied her swimming eyes and grimaced, feeling guilty without reason. 'You love them.'

'But, unfortunately, my love doesn't have a value in the same way because Eloise and Jack are still young enough to forget me and learn to love other people.' Freddie sighed in grudging acknowledgement of that reality. 'I would have to be contributing a lot more...and I don't have more yet there's nothing I *wouldn't* do to keep them!'

Zac watched tears trickle down her taut cheeks, tears she wasn't even aware that she was shedding because she was resolutely swigging the coffee she had got herself and keeping on talking earnestly, struggling to politely hide her anguish. He wished his mother had been capable of feeling even half as much after she had left him as a little boy marooned on the *fazenda* month after month, year after year, living in hope of visits or phone calls that had rarely happened. But, sadly for him, Antonella had craved her husband's child and no other and in all the years that had followed fate had only given her Zac and an endless stream of miscarriages and other disappointments.

There's nothing I wouldn't *do to keep them.*

The words echoed afresh in Zac's mind. And a subtle illuminating shift took place in his attitude at that point as a recollection of his father's advice surfaced simultaneously: choose a woman who at least *wants* a child. His lean, strong face tensed and shadowed. How was he to view a woman willing to make any sacrifice to keep children that were not even hers?

'You must love children,' Zac commented with forced casualness.

'I don't know about that,' Freddie demurred uncertainly. 'But I loved Eloise from the minute she was born…and Jack. He had to be weaned off drugs before he was allowed to leave hospital and I was so worried about his development at first but he's done so very well.'

'Jack's full of life,' Zac agreed lazily, deep in thought and struggling against so unfamiliar an exercise. He had skimmed along the shallow surface of life for a very long time, having learned far too young that caring too much about anything, wanting anything too much and setting hopes too high invariably hurt like hell. An intelligent man, therefore, should avoid optimistic goals, emotional entanglements and complications.

He needed a child. Freddie, however, needed a husband, willing to take on two children. The prospect of being a parent to *three* children shattered Zac and drew him up short in his ruminations. To adopt Eloise and Jack, he would definitely have to marry Freddie and meet all conventional expectations to satisfy the authorities involved and it would scarcely be an easy process. In all likelihood that process would also be hedged with regulations likely to curtail his every move. Was he prepared to go to such punitive lengths to solve his inheritance problem?

After all, he could choose virtually any woman to have his child. Zac had few illusions about his own worth on the matrimonial front. He was filthy rich and ambitious women targeted men who could provide a fantasy lifestyle. But in spite of being poor, Freddie didn't seem mercenary. In fact, she had infuriating principles set in stone that had held Zac to ransom and actually forced *him* into retreat. He didn't do caring and commitment, but he also knew that any child would require caring and commitment from him to thrive. He could *try* to meet those obligations though, couldn't he? He was not so divorced from humanity that change was impossible, he told himself stubbornly.

Zac focussed on Freddie, tousled dark blonde hair skimming her taut cheekbones, dark chocolate eyes surrounded by wet clogged eyelashes, which signally failed to diminish her appeal. Raw hunger rippled through him, hot as a river of lava, pushing and pulling at him even though he was far too shaken by the concept of becoming a father of three to really want to continue.

'When you finish work tonight, come up to the penthouse and we'll talk,' Zac murmured almost hoarsely through clenched teeth. 'There's a possibility that I could be able to help you retain custody of Eloise and Jack.'

Dumbfounded by that claim, which had come at her out of nowhere, Freddie stared in bewilderment back at him, her full pink lips parting in surprise to show pearly teeth. 'How?' she asked baldly.

'We'll discuss that later.' Zac dealt her a brooding appraisal. 'But I can tell you now that it'll come down to how much you're willing to give up to hang onto those kids.'

Freddie's gaze had widened. *'Anything.'*

'People often say stuff like that but they don't really mean it,' Zac dismissed with a sceptical glance. 'We'll talk about it and see if we can help each other.'

'Help each other?' she queried in wonderment.

Zac compressed his wide sensual mouth and finished his black coffee, refusing to expand on the topic.

In a complete daze, Freddie went back to work and watched Zac stride out of the bar twenty minutes later without even looking her way. How could he possibly help her? And how could she possibly help *him*? Her mind whirled with fantastical supposition, none of which made sense or seemed remotely likely. Meanwhile she was conscious of the stares of her co-workers and a new disturbing wariness in their attitude towards her.

'Obviously he's nailing her and you can't blame her, can you? I'd have him in a heartbeat!' one of the bar staff was opining when Freddie entered the locker room after work to change.

A horrible silence fell when her presence was noted and the other two women got very busy with their lockers before leaving in haste. Freddie's face was burning but such speculation was only to be expected. Of course, the staff was gossiping about Zac's apparent interest in her, and his intervention earlier on her behalf had only encouraged conjecture. Naturally everyone would assume that she was having sex with him. And if Zac had had anything to do with it, she thought ruefully, she would have been. No, it would have happened only once, she reasoned, unable to imagine that any more enduring relationship would have developed between them. Zac bore all the hallmarks of a man who got easily bored.

She slid through the door that communicated with the hotel foyer, her cheeks warm with discomfiture. She was shabbily dressed, a hoodie pulled on over her top and skinny jeans and sneakers in place of the shorts and high heels. She had put some concealer over her swollen eyes and she was depressingly conscious that she looked tired and washed out. She entered the lift Zac had used and a burly man in a suit stepped in straight after her and stuck a card in a slot.

'The penthouse?' he queried, looking her over doubtfully. 'Miss Lassiter?'

'Yes.'

'Mr da Rocha is expecting you,' he informed her as the doors closed. 'I'm Marco, one of his security team, and I work for him.'

Freddie realised that the private lift would not have worked for her without that all important card. When the lift stopped Marco led the way, opening the door to the penthouse and standing back for her to enter before closing the door on her heels. A door inside the suite opened and Zac strolled out, half naked, a pair of jeans hanging loose and unbuttoned on his lean hips.

'Oh, it's you. Make yourself at home,' he urged casually. 'Pour yourself a drink.'

And with that careless suggestion he stalked back barefoot into the bedroom, leaving her breathless because Zac half naked was an unforgettable sight: an expanse of ripped, incredibly muscled torso liberally inked with intricate designs leading down to a V of muscle that emphasised his flat, hard stomach and his narrow waist. Flustered and more nervous than ever, she tugged off her hoodie because she was too warm, and finger-combed her hair before approaching the well-stocked bar and choosing a juice. She was very grateful that he hadn't hung around long enough to notice that she had been welded to the floor and staring at him like an awestricken schoolgirl.

Annoyance that she was so easily overwhelmed by Zac's sheer impact licked at her. Yes, he was utterly, absolutely gorgeous but surely she was capable of acting normally around him? Had she *ever* acted normally around him? She didn't think she had. From that very first glimpse, he had unsettled her, then he had outraged her and from that point on she had become nervous, judgemental and oversensitive in his radius.

Zac reappeared fully dressed in a black shirt and jeans. His attention went straight to the glass in her hand. 'Tomato juice…*really*?'

'Alcohol would send me to sleep at this time of night,' she said defensively.

'I was teasing,' Zac assured her while he studied her and asked himself if access to her was worth what he would be sacrificing. Of course, it wouldn't be, his intelligence told him. No woman would ever be worth his freedom. But he had to be practical and work with the system, and if he married her and she didn't conceive his lawyers would be able to move to break the trust. One way or another marriage would be a step forward and he would move closer to his goal of complete independence and control of the diamond mines that were his family heritage.

'Why did you say that we might be able to help each other?' Freddie pressed tautly.

Zac settled down carelessly opposite her on the arm of a sofa and leant back, wide shoulders squared, long, powerful thighs spread and braced. 'I'm the heir to the Quintal da Rocha diamond mines. I receive the profits but I won't be able to control the business until I have produced an heir of my own. That iniquitous arrangement was laid down in a legal trust by my great-great-grandfather a long time ago and I deeply resent it.'

'You *have* to have a child?' Freddie whispered with disconcerted emphasis.

'Yes, and if you are willing to try and give me that child *I* am willing to marry you and attempt to adopt Eloise and Jack with you,' Zac completed smoothly.

The mention of marriage shocked Freddie so much that she took a great desperate gulp of her tomato juice and almost choked on it, coughing and then clearing her throat with a painful swallow while Zac continued to steadily watch her. 'You'd be willing to adopt Eloise and Jack?' she prompted shakily, careening wildly from one thought to the next, all her thoughts disjointed and incomplete.

'If you also agree to meet my condition by giving me a child,' Zac responded with measured cool.

'Do you have a criminal record?' Freddie demanded, disconcerting him with the staggering abruptness of that question.

Ebony brows drew together in perplexity. 'Of course not.'

Freddie went pink. 'Just asking. You probably couldn't be considered as an adoptive parent with a record.'

Zac was entertained by that tactless leap-frogging question that revealed that she was already considering his proposition. 'Have you ever been pregnant?' he traded in return.

Freddie stiffened and shook her head. 'Er...no, I'm afraid, no proven fertility record here.'

Zac lifted and dropped a fatalistic shoulder. 'Either of us could be infertile. At this point, it doesn't really matter because I have to go through the motions...marry and *try* to have a child, and if it doesn't happen for us I can then go to court and ask for the trust to be set aside.'

'You would *truly* be prepared to adopt Eloise and Jack with me?' Freddie prompted, sudden tears burning the backs of her eyes at the idea that there could possibly be a solution that would enable her to keep her sister's children.

'Yes, if you agree. You said you'd do anything to keep them and I will also pretty much do anything it takes to gain control of the da Rocha business empire,' Zac admitted grimly.

As if she had been winded by a feverish sprint, Freddie coiled back almost bonelessly into the sofa and snatched in a deep shuddering breath, striving to calm down and think with clarity. She had to set down her glass because her hand was shaking so badly. 'Do you think we'd have a chance of adopting the kids together?' she asked anxiously, refusing to plunge herself into the turmoil of considering what it would be like to marry Zac and have a child with him and instead concentrating on what was most important to her at that moment.

'I don't see why not if we present ourselves as a loving couple. I'm wealthy enough to buy us a home. I'm also mixed race, like the children.'

'Are you?' Freddie studied him in surprise.

'My grandmother on my mother's side is black. My grandfather was white,' Zac explained. 'Brazil is a huge melting pot of ethnic diversity and if you're like me you can't choose your genes when you reproduce. I'm telling you that now because any child we have could take after either side of my family.'

Freddie nodded understanding.

'Not every woman could comfortably accept that possibility,' Zac admitted, involuntarily amused by Freddie's complete lack of reaction to his frankness.

His mother had been haunted by the spectre of her husband's racism and her fear of having a child of a darker complexion than her own while Zac had been relentlessly bullied at an almost exclusively white school for being the only child that was different. He had learned to fight to protect himself at an early age, but he had also had to learn how to back down when there were too many ranged against him. The trouble that had erupted around Zac then had led to him being labelled an agitator, a tag he had fiercely resented.

Silence fell while Zac surveyed Freddie, coiling tendrils of lust curling up hotly through him. He remembered the rounded little curve of her bottom in the shorts, the shapely length of her legs, and pictured her spread across his bed in various different positions, anticipation and hunger leaping through his veins. He could not remember *ever* wanting a woman with such fierce immediacy. Had her reluctance sustained his desire? Was he truly so basic that he needed the challenge she had represented? And why did the idea of getting her pregnant turn him on as hard and fast as a bullet? Wasn't that a little kinky? A hard line of colour suffused his exotic, high cheekbones and, sliding upright, he strode over to the bar to pour himself a drink.

'Not for me, thanks,' Freddie framed when he glanced at her enquiringly.

'You're very quiet,' he murmured warily.

'Shocked,' Freddie contradicted. 'Marriage...seriously, you and me?'

'Not a for-ever kind of marriage,' Zac qualified softly. 'But I would still continue to be involved in the children's lives, regardless of what happens between us.'

The marriage would not be permanent, Freddie interpreted, but he was still promising that he would go on being a father to the children. Obviously he was planning on an eventual divorce to regain his freedom, leaving her a single parent with three children. A child with Zac, *having* a child with Zac, she grasped suddenly, her face and body gripped by heat at the notion. She stared down at her feet, shutting out that silly flush of sexual awareness and exasperated by it, because just then it struck her as a trivial issue when compared to the awful threat of losing her sister's children, whom she loved and who had learned to love her. Sex was no big deal, she told herself urgently. Sex would *have* to be no big deal if they were forced to try and conceive a child because that could take months and months to achieve. The alternative would be to lose Eloise and Jack, whom she could not bear to imagine her life without. That recollection steadied her nerves and cooled her down. She had to keep on reminding herself of what the end result of such an arrangement would be.

'Is divorce a stumbling block for you?' Zac prompted with a frown.

'No. But this idea of yours…well, it's a lot to get my head around,' she confided ruefully, cheeks colouring as she encountered his pale glittering gaze, finally recognising how very intense he could be because she could feel the raw force of his volatile temperament in that assessing appraisal.

'You said you'd do anything,' he reminded her sibilantly.

'Marriage and a baby?' Freddie quipped. 'Not something I'd even got around to thinking about yet.'

'If we married, you would also be financially secure for life. You would never have to work again if you didn't want to,' Zac continued.

And even though she knew he was trying to tempt her, she was filled with anticipation of what her life could be like were she free to live it and have sufficient money to afford childcare. She had missed out on her place at college, where she had planned to train as a teacher, because after finding Eloise cold, wet and hungry in her cot, forgotten by Lauren, she had known that there was no way she could leave a baby alone with her sister. Not when Eloise needed her, not when Freddie loved Eloise as much as if she had given birth to her herself. Those were the truths that had reshaped Freddie's future and forced tough, unselfish choices on her.

'All I want is what's best for the children. That has to be my main aim,' Freddie declared. 'You'd have to start taking the time to get to know them properly.'

'I'll do whatever it takes. I want you—'

'For a while,' Freddie interposed ironically, brown velvet eyes flickering over his lean, darkly handsome features, her mouth running dry. 'And I come as a package with two children. I don't want them damaged in any way by *our* choices.'

'We're only human. We can't see the future but my motivation is good. I don't want anyone harmed by this arrangement.'

'But why did you pick me?' she asked baldly.

'I can be businesslike about this with you because you have as much to gain from the marriage as I do,' Zac stated. 'I like that because it gives us a better chance of making it work. *Com certeza*…of course, if I wasn't attracted to you, it wouldn't work on any level.'

Freddie reddened, lashes cloaking her gaze as she tore her attention from his lean, powerful figure, her body slowly heating. Her nipples prickled and tightened, her thighs pressing tightly together to ease the sudden compulsive ache between them. Wanting without any hope of satisfaction hurt, she finally acknowledged, but she still tensed at the prospect of giving way to that need.

But Zac was offering her what she wanted in return for what he wanted and she deemed it a fair bargain if he was willing to take on parenting her niece and nephew and any child they had of their own. She concentrated on the positives. Zac would give them security. Zac would be another parent to support her. After a while he would not be around on a daily basis as a father, but in a world where nothing was certain and marriages often broke down that was not unusual and at least he was being honest about his intentions from the outset.

She didn't have an alternative choice. Nobody else was coming to rescue her. And even Zac wasn't rescuing her, she reflected wryly. He was offering her a lifebelt on one hand and demanding his pound of flesh with the other. They would be equal partners in the marriage because both of them would be bringing something important to the table. Would she be able to conceive? How long would it take to accomplish that feat? And what would it feel like to have Zac as a husband and lover and then lose him again? But all those scary questions were for the future and not relevant to the present.

'Yes. I am attracted to you,' she said stiffly, reckoning that there was no longer any need to pretend otherwise.

A wide appreciative grin slashed Zac's mouth. 'No more lies, then.'

'No more lies,' she agreed ruefully. 'I'm saying yes to your proposition because you're the only hope I have of keeping Eloise and Jack and I'll do whatever I have to do to facilitate that.'

'*Venha aqui*…come here,' Zac urged.

Stiff as a plank of wood, Freddie rose from her

seat and approached him. He swept her up like a doll and held her high with the kind of controlled physical strength that shook her. 'You won't regret this decision,' he told her and then he kissed her.

Hotly, extravagantly, passionately and with all the energy that drove him, he crushed her soft lips beneath his, both arms banded so tightly round her narrow ribcage that she could barely breathe. But she didn't want to breathe, she just wanted to fall deeper into that kiss. His tongue ravaged the tender interior of her mouth and a shower of sparks flew up inside her, tingling along every nerve ending in her slender body. His tongue teased and flicked and darted and with a gasp she closed her arms dizzily round his neck.

'We could get this project off to a flying start right now,' Zac suggested thickly.

And Freddie froze and let go of him, pushing him away until he had to let her down to stand on her own feet again.

'Problem?' Zac quipped very drily, his eyes luminous and coolly enquiring in the dim lights.

'I'm not getting into bed with you until we're legally married,' Freddie spelt out in a defiant rush as she fought for what little security she could retain, which to her meant staying safe and uncommitted to the last possible moment. 'You could still be shooting me a crazy seduction line. After all, you *are* the guy who bets sports cars away! I won't take the risk of getting pregnant until you've proved your commitment to our agreement.'

Zac stared at her in astonishment. 'You think this could be a scam?' he breathed incredulously, astonished by the level of her distrust. 'I've never had to seduce a woman in my life!'

Freddie backed away another few steps, embarrassed now that she had voiced her reservations. 'I'm naturally suspicious—'

'Of men,' Zac slotted in boldly. 'You don't trust my sex.'

'My past experiences have not been good,' Freddie conceded reluctantly.

'Then tomorrow we'll get this party started with a visit to my London lawyers. They'll make a start on the adoption application and advise us on how soon we can get married here. Bring your birth certificate and your passport and the children's,' Zac advised, his lean, hard-boned face set with purpose.

Freddie groaned out loud. 'Zac… I don't have a passport and neither do the children. In any case the authorities wouldn't allow us to take the children out of the UK without their permission.'

'You've never been abroad?' Zac asked in astonishment.

'Never,' Freddie confirmed.

'My lawyers will deal with all the details,' Zac pronounced with innate arrogance.

'And I'll have the children in tow,' Freddie warned. 'And they can't go on a motorbike.'

'Obviously not,' Zac fielded drily. 'Stop putting obstacles in my path, *meu pequenino*. When I want something, I allow nothing to get in my way…and I *want* you.'

Freddie went pink, disconcerted by that unequivocal statement of intent. And yet in the strangest way she found his determination to have her ridiculously flattering, because no man had ever wanted her with such stubborn, resolute intensity. Of course that wouldn't last, she told herself ruefully, not once he realised how inexperienced and ordinary she was. No doubt he was expecting fireworks in the bedroom. How would he feel when he instead wakened to find Eloise and Jack in bed with them at some ungodly hour of the morning? Family life, she thought heavily, was likely to be a big culture shock for Zac.

CHAPTER FIVE

'IT'S PERFECT,' ZAC pronounced as Freddie smoothed an apprehensive finger down over the knee-length, shimmering silver sheath dress.

'But what does it cost?' Freddie hissed in an anxious undertone, fearful of attracting the attention of the saleswoman, who was grander than a queen.

Zac dealt her a silencing look that was equally intimidating. Requesting prices was apparently a vulgar act in his radius. Apparently, prices were no longer her business but *his*. Freddie sucked in a steadying breath but it didn't work. From the instant she had agreed to marry Zac, her life had begun changing at warp speed.

The next morning, he had taken her straight into a meeting with his London lawyers. Freddie had tried to keep Eloise and Jack entertained in a corner while incomprehensible legal jargon interwoven with long voluble snatches of Portuguese had whirled round the room. Zac had made copious notes on his phone and dragged her out of there again, but only after she had filled in a sheaf of official documents. They had climbed back into the limousine that had picked them up that morning, a real genuine long black limousine complete with car seats for the children, and that was the first time Freddie had actually come to terms with the idea that Zac was very rich.

New experience after new experience had bombarded her ever since and she felt dizzy from the shock of it all. Without the children around to ground her, she felt lost. Claire had agreed to keep Eloise and Jack while they went shopping for a new outfit for Freddie. Zac had wanted to hire a nanny and had been exasperated when he had finally grasped that only Claire was officially allowed to take care of the children. That was Zac, infuriated by red tape and rules, always impatient to move quickly past them to the next challenge.

A giant blue diamond solitaire ring weighed down Freddie's left hand and if she stirred even a finger it sparkled with blinding brilliance. It was a very beautiful and eye-catching ring.

'Play everything by the book,' Zac's legal team had advised him, and that seemed to entail doing stuff that Zac's unconventional heart rebelled against. He had been told to give her an engagement ring, introduce her to his family and play up his family connections, not one of which acts came naturally to him. So, Freddie could not feel flattered by anything Zac had done or arranged although she was grateful that he was willing to do it to facilitate their application to adopt Eloise and Jack.

'You do what you *have* to do,' Zac had enunciated through gritted teeth as he had slid that extraordinarily opulent ring onto her ring finger.

No, there had been no risk of Freddie suspecting that Zac cherished more romantic feelings for her than he was willing to share with her. And shopping with him even for one morning was a bit of a nightmare for a shy, introverted young woman. Evidently, he liked women clad in skimpy lingerie, and he had been wildly disconcerted by her mortification when he had discussed *his* preferences for what she was to wear with the saleswoman. More than ever, it had made Freddie feel as though she was just a body to Zac, a body for him to dress and impregnate at the same speed with which he did everything else. That very evening they were joining his family for what he had described as 'an informal dinner'. Yet the event obviously required her to wear a designer dress with all the trimmings.

'Those shoes,' Zac indicated to the hovering assistant with a careless sweep of one bronzed hand. 'That bag.'

'You *have* to get more into the spirit of this,' Zac censured as he herded her back out to the limousine like a wayward sheep, who might stray. 'You've got a fitting for your wedding dress tomorrow.'

Two days earlier, Freddie had chosen the dress in a

breathtakingly impressive designer atelier while Zac had turned Jack upside down to keep him amused and strings of baby chuckles had filled the air and Eloise had stood by awaiting her turn.

'I don't see why it matters what I wear when I meet your family,' Freddie admitted. 'It's not as if you even want me to meet them!'

'I'm not close to my half-brothers but over time that could change, particularly when all of us have young children. I would like the connection for *our* children,' Zac admitted with emphasis. 'Growing up, I had virtually no family and it made me a loner. I want the kids to have a different experience. And it *does* matter what you wear when you meet my family.'

'How?'

'Angel's wife, Merry, and my father's girlfriend, Sybil, will look as if they walked straight off a Paris catwalk. I will not have you look *less* than them in any way,' Zac completed grimly, his pride on the line. No way would he allow Freddie to be patronised or labelled unfit for such exclusive company. Without effort she would outshine all of them, he thought with satisfaction, surveying her delicate triangular face and her warm brown eyes.

She would be the perfect wife for him, he savoured. She wouldn't be clingy or needy because she would be far too wrapped up in the children to worry about what he was doing. She wouldn't make demands or throw temperamental jealous or possessive tantrums. She would just get on with things the way he did without making a big song and dance about them. Freddie was wonderfully practical, so she wouldn't go falling for him or anything inconvenient like that either. She had already signed the pre-nuptial agreement without the smallest difficulty. 'A woman in a million,' one of his lawyers had commented afterwards and Zac had felt very real pride in his future wife, who was so gloriously free of avarice and ambition.

Unaware of the unspoken accolades coming her way, Freddie settled into a corner of the opulent limo and studied Zac's lean, darkly handsome face. He looked so different from the man she had first met. He had abandoned his jeans and worn sharply tailored suits for all their official appointments and, ironically, he wore a suit with the panache of one born to such formality. Exquisitely tailored in a fine grey wool and silk blend, his present dark grey suit outlined his broad shoulders and wide chest and enhanced his lean hips and long powerful legs to perfection. In jeans he looked incredibly masculine and sexy but in a suit he was to die for.

Her body was all of a quiver in his radius because it didn't matter how much he annoyed or confused her, he still fascinated her. Her temperature rose, her heartbeat quickened, her sensitive breasts feeling constricted by her bra. She pressed her slender jeans-clad thighs together tightly, struggling to contain the swelling heat at the heart of her.

'Don't look at me like that,' Zac husked. 'Not when you don't want me to do anything about it.'

Freddie turned pink, striving to look inviting and flirtatious rather than desperate to be touched. 'You can still kiss me.'

'No, I can't,' Zac contradicted. 'I won't start anything we can't finish. I've already had enough cold showers to last me a lifetime.'

That blunt response sent a tide of hot colour washing up over her disconcerted face. Her eyes evaded the allure of his glittering and all too compelling light grey gaze. Something tightened low in her pelvis, a contracting thread of very physical yearning that was strong enough to unnerve her.

'You can't *still* believe that I'm going to jilt you at the altar,' Zac intoned thickly.

Freddie swallowed with difficulty. 'Not any more,' she conceded reluctantly.

'Then come back to the penthouse with me tonight. I'm dying here.' Zac groaned that feeling admission without a shade of inhibition. 'I've never gone without sex for as long as this.'

'I'd prefer not to,' she muttered tightly, that gruff, innately sexual intonation making her body burn hotly from head to toe. 'Because it'll be my first time and I just think it'll feel more relaxed once we're married.'

Zac frowned, ebony brows drawing together. 'Your first time at what?' he queried.

'At sex,' Freddie framed, her soft pink lips compressing with embarrassment.

Zac looked back at her, stunned, the riddle Freddie had occasionally shown herself to be suddenly clarified. 'You're a virgin…a *virgin*?' he said again as if she now fell into the same unlikely category as a unicorn. 'Are you joking?'

'No,' she confirmed flatly.

'OK.' Zac rolled his eyes, attempting to compute this new information and utterly failing because he was so startled. 'But *why* are you still a virgin?' he persisted.

'I don't want to talk about that, right now,' Freddie told him hastily, hugely relieved to see that the limo had come to a halt near Claire's terraced home and that escape into the company of others, where even Zac could not continue such a conversation, was within reach.

'You can hardly blame me for being surprised,' Zac murmured in reproof. 'I had no idea.'

'It's not something I feel a need to talk about,' Freddie parried in frustration.

And Zac looked back to their very first meeting and barely managed to suppress a groan of frustration. Without even knowing it he had blown his chances with her right from the start by assuming that she would be as laid-back and casual about sex as he was. Now he knew differently, now he knew why her barriers went up the instant he got too close, but he still could not even begin to understand why she had retained her inexperience into her twenties. It was a complication he hadn't expected and he didn't know how he felt about it. But obviously, any plans to enjoy a sexual marathon to satisfy his currently rampant libido would be out of the question.

Eloise and Jack engulfed him in the narrow hallway. Jack clutched at his knees and Zac hoisted the baby high, ruffling Eloise's hair as she sucked her thumb and rested her head sleepily against his thigh. The kids were so trusting and openly affectionate with him that it touched even his hard heart. Claire had said enough for him to know that Freddie had dealt with a lot of stuff she shouldn't have had to deal with in an effort to shield the children from lasting damage at her sister's hands. But Zac was beginning to recognise the damage done to Freddie, who, like a victim of abuse, was very nervous around men and found it very hard to trust.

'I took them to the park,' Claire told Freddie. 'They're exhausted and ready for a nap.'

'I'll take them upstairs,' Freddie volunteered.

'Want the dragon story,' Eloise mumbled round her thumb, clutching at Zac's jacket.

Over the past two weeks, Zac had not left the house without having to read the dragon story at least once and he gave way with grace, shepherding

Eloise into the lounge where she quickly produced her favourite book. Jack went to sleep on his shoulder while Zac read and then Eloise announced her desire to go to the zoo to see a real dragon. Zac explained that dragons flew so fast and high in the sky that zookeepers couldn't catch them. Eloise looked sad but cheered up when Zac reminded her that he was taking them to the zoo with Claire the next day while Freddie had her dress fitting.

Freddie watched and marvelled at the noticeable bond even now forming between Zac and her niece and nephew. Their interaction was very comfortable. Both she and Zac had already had initial interviews with social services and character references and basic documentation had been lodged. With their wedding only forty-eight hours away, Freddie believed that everything was progressing as well as could be expected. Zac had also requested permission to apply for passports for the children and to take them abroad for a trip after the wedding.

Claire had said that they were crazy to jump into marriage so fast simply in the hope of adopting the two children. Freddie had kept Zac's need for a child of his own to herself, leaving the brunette to assume that Zac had fallen madly in love with her and she with him. And in truth, Freddie reckoned that she would've fallen for Zac had he not made such a disastrously bad first impression on her. Now when she saw him entertaining the children even for a few minutes, she blessed the quirk of fate that had brought him into their lives, for without him where would she have been? In despair at the threat of losing the children she loved.

Even so, she was nervous as anything at the prospect of meeting Zac's rich and fancy relatives and their undoubtedly high standards. At least the royal pair would not be present, she thought with relief. Apparently, Prince Vitale's mother had abdicated after a huge scandal and, now that Vitale was about to become King, he and his pregnant wife were much too involved in official business to spare the time for a family dinner in London.

With such grand people in the family, would Zac's lofty relatives criticise her the moment she was out of hearing? Would they be shocked by his choice of someone like her? Would they try to persuade him to change his mind at the last minute and *not* marry her? After all, a waitress with two children in tow was no great catch for a very wealthy and educated man. She would never be his equal in the eyes of the world. Perhaps they would simply shake their heads in surprise and remind themselves that Zac needed an heir and that it might as well be Freddie as any other woman. Perhaps they simply wouldn't care either way.

That evening, Zac long gone and the children readied for bed, Freddie got dressed for the dinner she was dreading with Zac's father and his girlfriend and his elder brother and his wife. It bothered her that he had told her so little about himself and she worried that she would stumble in conversation and reveal her ignorance.

Zac stood at the passenger door of the limo watching Freddie descend the steps, her tiny feet in pearlised shoes, ultra-careful in the high heels, her clutch pinned between white-knuckled fingers, her state of nerves patent. But she looked absolutely amazing, like a delicate doll in silver, shapely legs as fragile as the rest of her, big brown eyes anxiously pinned to him.

'You look fantastic,' he told her bracingly, wishing she weren't a virgin, wishing he could lower the privacy shields and pounce on her in the car to live out every fantasy she had awakened. But intelligence warned him to hang onto his self-control. She would trot out all sorts of excuses when he finally tackled her but Zac had already reached his own conclusions: she was *scared* of sex, *scared* of everything he made her feel. The last thing she needed from him was *more* pressure. He would have to be rather more subtle than nature had made him if he didn't want to risk frightening her off.

'Thanks,' she said tautly, settling into the limo to fiddle unnecessarily with her clutch bag while studiously avoiding his attention. 'So, your father married twice and that's where Angel and Vitale come from but he had an affair with your mother and she was in love with someone else.'

Zac lounged back with a sigh. 'Both Charles and Antonella were on the rebound when they met in Brazil. If Afonso hadn't returned to my mother, Charles would've married her as soon as he was free to do so. My father seems to fall in love with every woman he sleeps with. He's a very tender-hearted man.'

'But your mother still loved your stepfather even though he treated her so badly? I mean, ditching her when they were engaged to go off with another woman?' Freddie prompted in surprise, stealing a glance at him, loving how elegant he was in his dinner jacket. Clean-shaven for once without a hint of his usual stubble, his perfect features were revealed from the smooth planes of his high cheekbones to the strong angle of his jawline. His deep-set heavily lashed light eyes gleamed and, caught staring, she reddened, her mouth running dry, all concentration evaporating simultaneously.

Zac shrugged. 'I never understood her obsession but Afonso Oliveira was *it* for my mother. She worshipped the ground he walked on and believed he had done a wonderful thing in overlooking her humble background to choose her as a wife.'

'How was her background humble when she was born into so much wealth?' Freddie asked in disbelief.

'She was the illegitimate daughter of a black maid and some people, notably those of my stepfather's ilk, looked down on her for that. My grandfather ignored my mother's existence because he was equally snobbish. Afonso was from a similar aristocratic background. The Oliveiras had long since run through their family fortune but that was less important than their reputation and their impressive family tree.'

'Your mother had a sad life.' Freddie sighed reflectively. 'She didn't really fit anywhere.'

'Life is what you make of it. Her attachment to Afonso was toxic. Getting too attached to anyone is dangerous,' Zac pronounced grimly. 'Think of how attached you are to Eloise and Jack and the sacrifices you're prepared to make to keep them!'

Unexpectedly, Freddie smiled. 'But, loving them has enriched my life in so many other ways. Yes, I could have made different choices but they're my family and they make me happy. I have no regrets.'

The dinner was being held in a private room at an exclusive restaurant. Freddie remembered Charles Russell and his eldest son, Angel, joining Zac for coffee one morning. But the two women, one brunette and one elegant, much older blonde, were completely new to her. The blonde turned out to be Sybil, Charles' girlfriend and also, it seemed, Merry's grandmother.

Zac kept one arm wrapped protectively round Freddie's spine as he introduced her to everyone.

Angel's wife, Merry, admired Freddie's ring, but although both women were charming Merry seemed a little uncomfortable around Freddie and Zac, while Zac's father treated Freddie for all the world as though she was his dream choice of bride for his youngest son.

They took their seats while Freddie noted what the other two women were wearing and recognised that Zac had not brought her to the party overdressed. Merry and Sybil sparkled with jewellery and sported stylish outfits sprinkled with the kind of little handmade embellishments that screamed haute couture. Merry talked about her little girl and asked her about Eloise and Jack. Zac shared Eloise's current obsession with dragons. Charles was asking when he could hope to meet the children when Freddie rose at the last minute to follow the other two women out to the cloakroom.

'I just felt *so* awkward meeting Freddie!' Merry was exclaiming loudly in the corridor as she and her grandmother rounded a corner. 'I wish Jazz hadn't told me what Zac got up to at the royal ball.'

'What did he get up to?' the older woman asked as Freddie automatically speeded up in the hope of hearing the rest of the tantalising exchange.

'Apparently, Zac disappeared into a private room with two women that work at the palace. Obviously, they went in there to have sex. Jazz said he didn't even blush when he reappeared. He's shameless,'

Merry contended in a pained voice. 'But that was only two weeks ago. How am I supposed to treat Freddie like a happy bride-to-be when I know that Zac was still playing away so recently?'

'Well, I think you have to give Zac the benefit of the doubt because only the individuals in that room know what actually happened there. I also think you need to remind yourself that you are very happy with a man who enjoyed an equally raunchy reputation *before* he married you,' the other woman commented wryly.

Snatching in a breath, Freddie had frozen where she stood as she listened. Merry and her grandmother were talking about Zac. Apparently, he had had sex with two women at the Lerovian ball that Freddie had declined to attend. *Two* women. Shock rippled like a lightning bolt through Freddie, jarring every bone and muscle. A wave of fierce jealousy ripped through her in the aftermath as she realised that, without ever thinking too deeply about it, she had come to look on Zac as *hers*. Yet while coming on to *her*, pretending to want *her*, he had still been having sex with other women. That knowledge cut into her like a knife and made her feel like a fool. How many other women had he dallied with since they met? Appalled and deeply wounded, she walked stiffly into the cloakroom as the other women were leaving and managed a vague smile even though she felt like a zombie.

How could she marry a man she couldn't even trust to be faithful? She had taken exclusivity for granted in their relationship but it was not something they had actually discussed. She had made stupid, naïve assumptions, she acknowledged painfully, and Zac had played on her lack of experience. Telling her that he had never gone so long without sex! Yet it was only two weeks since the ball. Was two weeks a long time for him? How did she know? And what did she care? How could she possibly care about a man that brazen?

Thankfully, she didn't *care* about him, she told herself resolutely. She was wildly attracted to him but that was all, because she was cautious with her feelings and careful to protect herself from unhealthy attachments. She had watched, after all, what love did to her sister, Lauren. Lauren had bent every rule there was to justify keeping Cruz in her life, refusing to break away from him, excusing his infidelities as a trifling 'man thing'.

Zac noticed how pale and quiet Freddie was when she returned to the table and decided that it was time to call it a night. She was probably tired, he thought wryly, knowing the kids woke her at the crack of dawn. He had seen the tiny room she shared with the children and marvelled that she could live in that confined space without complaint. He draped an arm round her as they said their good-byes, but she pulled away from him on the pavement outside, slipping into the waiting limo like a little silvery ghost.

'Can we go back to the hotel first?' Freddie asked tautly. 'We have to talk.'

Angel had once joked that the four deadliest words in Merry's vocabulary were those words but Zac was nonchalant, cocooned as he was in his conviction that he was absolutely without a sin to his name. He wondered only absently what she wanted to talk about.

CHAPTER SIX

'NO, THANKS,' FREDDIE said flatly in answer to the offer of a drink.

Zac was already revising his belief that nothing could be seriously amiss because Freddie was posed in front of him with all the accusing stiffness and tension of a miniature St Joan of Arc. All she lacked was a sword and a burning torch. 'What's happening here?' he demanded abruptly.

'I overheard a conversation tonight,' Freddie volunteered between gritted teeth, struggling to prevent herself from visibly trembling with rage. 'I heard how you entertained yourself at the royal ball.'

Zac put the evidence together and within seconds he had the whole picture clear in his mind. Vitale's wife, Jazz, had probably gossiped to Merry and then Merry had talked and somehow Freddie had got to listen. His macho pride had been his downfall, he registered, his teeth gritting. Losing the bet, not even being able to persuade Freddie to join him at the ball, had hit his ego hard and when his brothers had assumed he was partaking of a little al fresco sex, he had seen no reason to put the record straight.

Now Freddie had judged him and found him wanting and it was far from the first time he had endured the experience of others believing the worst of him. As a child he had come up with his own defence strategy and it had only hardened to steel as he matured. Never apologise, never explain. In point of fact he didn't owe Freddie any explanations as they had not been together at the time. He had done nothing he was ashamed of doing. He had told no lies, had caused no injury to anyone and he refused to apologise for something he hadn't done to keep the peace.

If Freddie was going to be his wife, she had to respect his boundaries. He loathed emotional blackmail and had no scruples about fighting fire with fire.

'Was it educational?' Zac countered softly, his sibilant Brazilian accent roughening his vowel sounds with the hint that he might not be as cool and calm as he appeared.

His apparent complete lack of reaction infuriated Freddie. He stood there, lean, powerful body balanced and strong in his beautifully cut suit, his eyes glittering like crushed ice below his luxuriant black lashes.

'Is that all you've got to say to me?' Freddie launched at him furiously.

'I don't know what else I can say since you still haven't clarified the issue,' Zac responded with sardonic bite.

Colour spattered her cheeks, chasing away the pallor induced by shock. 'You went into a private room at the ball to have sex with two women.'

'No, that's incorrect,' Zac contradicted. 'I went into the room first to make a phone call and two women followed me in.'

'If you think that *that* makes a difference to *my* feelings—' Freddie began heatedly, incensed that he still seemed in absolute stress-free control. He wasn't embarrassed. He wasn't angry at being found out. He wasn't even defensive. And even worse, if he had a drop of guilt in him he wasn't showing it.

Zac threw his arrogant dark head back. 'That's how it happened, but I don't understand what your feelings have to do with it—'

'Oh, you don't, don't you?' Freddie broke in, almost bouncing on her high heels as she threw herself as tall as she could, slight shoulders squaring with hostility.

'No, I don't,' Zac repeated. 'We were not in a relationship at the time. In fact, forty-eight hours before the ball you walked out on me, making it clear that you wanted nothing more to do with me.'

That reminder flashed through Freddie like paraffin thrown on a bonfire and only sent the rage clawing up inside her climbing higher. 'You said you wanted *me* and then you went off and had sleazy sex with another woman the first opportunity you got!' she slung back at him in disgust.

'No, that wasn't the first opportunity,' Zac corrected with a reflective air and a cynical set to his sensual mouth. 'I was approached in the VIP lounge at the airport by a woman, propositioned by a stewardess on my flight and given at least two phone numbers after I landed in Lerovia. So, no, *not* my first opportunity to let loose.'

Freddie stared at him in mounting disbelief and horror. The one undeniable truth about Zac da Rocha was that he was gorgeous and many women didn't wait for him to demonstrate interest before going into pursuit. She had watched that happening in the bar when women became frustrated at failing to attract his attention and then made more aggressive moves. But the concrete proof that Zac was targeted by so many other women only sent Freddie plunging even deeper into panic mode. How could someone as ordinary as she was ever hope to hold onto the interest of such a spectacular male specimen? It was obvious that she could not and that getting out before she got in any deeper was her sole option.

'Fidelity is very, *very* important to me,' Freddie declared shakily, struggling to breathe evenly and stay calm even when she felt like an over-shaken cocktail of drama inside herself.

'Yet we're getting married the day after tomor-

Dear Reader,

IT'S A FACT: if you answer 4 quick questions, we'll send you 4 FREE REWARDS!

I'm not kidding you. As a leading publisher of women's fiction, we value your opinions… and your time. That's why we are prepared to **reward** you handsomely for completing our mini-survey. In fact, we have 4 Free Rewards for you, including 2 free books and 2 free gifts.

As you may have guessed, that's why our mini-survey is called **"4 for 4".** Answer 4 questions and get 4 Free Rewards. It's that simple!

Thank you for participating in our survey,

Pam Powers

To get your 4 FREE REWARDS:
Complete the survey below and return the insert today to receive 2 FREE BOOKS and 2 FREE GIFTS guaranteed!

▶ DETACH AND MAIL CARD TODAY!

"4 for 4" MINI-SURVEY

1 Is reading one of your favorite hobbies?
☐ YES ☐ NO

2 Do you prefer to read instead of watch TV?
☐ YES ☐ NO

3 Do you read newspapers and magazines?
☐ YES ☐ NO

4 Do you enjoy trying new book series with FREE BOOKS?
☐ YES ☐ NO

YES! I have completed the above Mini-Survey. Please send me my **4 FREE REWARDS** (worth over $20 retail). I understand that I am under no obligation to buy anything, as explained on the back of this card.

❏ I prefer the regular-print edition
106/306 HDL GMYF

❏ I prefer the larger-print edition
176/376 HDL GMYF

FIRST NAME	LAST NAME

ADDRESS

APT.#	CITY

STATE/PROV.	ZIP/POSTAL CODE

row and this is the first time you've mentioned it,' Zac pointed out, pouring himself a malt whiskey and tossing it back without hesitation because when it came to the issue of fidelity there was really nothing he wanted to say. He had never had to be faithful because he had never stayed long enough with any one woman for that to become a concern. But that confession would scarcely soothe Freddie.

'I just assumed...you know...' Freddie forced out the words because her throat was closing over and aching '...that I could trust you and now I've found out I *can't* trust you.'

Zac swung back to her, his lean, powerful limbs compellingly graceful in motion, stunning eyes like blazing polar stars, his anger unhidden now. 'We broke up before I even left for Lerovia. Anything I did there is my business. Obviously, I have a past. I can't change that.'

'This wasn't the past...this was only two weeks ago!' Freddie condemned stridently, fighting the tears threatening her, refusing to show weakness and break down. 'I can't marry a man I can't trust!'

'That is, of course, your decision but, considering that our marriage was supposed to be more based on practicality than sentiment, I don't see where the problem arises.'

'No, and the fact you *can't* see it only proves that we shouldn't marry!' Freddie threw back at him vehemently. 'You said you had never gone so long without sex and yet you were with other women only two weeks ago.'

Zac decided that he wasn't going to get involved in such dangerous trifles when she was acting like a rocket about to go off and light the night skies for miles around. Never apologise, never explain, he reminded himself stubbornly, angry with her, disappointed in her inability to cool down, face facts and see his point of view. She was in no fit state to grasp any explanation while she was still screaming at him. 'You need to calm down and think this through,' he murmured grimly, his firm sensual mouth compressing with steely self-control.

'I don't have to think about anything,' Freddie told him woodenly, misery creeping over her like a toxic cloud that shut out all the light. 'I can't marry an untrustworthy, unreliable womaniser. There's no coming back from that.'

'All that speech is telling me is that you have never been realistic about our marriage. Not only have you not recognised the boundaries I set, but you have also decided to judge me for sins I haven't committed,' Zac concluded grittily. 'Even so, when you fall off your soapbox I'll be waiting.'

'And that's all you've got to say to me?' Freddie ranted back at him, because she was far from finished and he was shutting her down.

'This is not a productive dialogue,' Zac growled,

yanking open the door for her departure. 'The car's waiting downstairs to take you home.'

And the pain didn't engulf Freddie until she climbed back into the car and slumped like a doll who had had the stuffing beaten out of her. She travelled from thwarted rage to devastated hurt in the space of seconds. So, it was over. She tasted the concept, reeled from it, wondered vaguely what else she had expected when she'd chosen to confront him. It had been too like a fairy tale anyway, she told herself... Zac coming along and seemingly offering her a lifeline when everything was falling apart.

When had anything that unexpectedly good ever happened to her before? She wasn't a lucky person, never had been. She hadn't been lucky when her parents died, hadn't been lucky when it came to getting Lauren off drugs and she had been even less lucky when it came to retaining custody of the children. And that was the moment when Freddie realised that she had forgotten where her niece and nephew fitted into their marriage plans. Aghast, she felt a chill running up over her entire body, driving out the heat of anger, bitterness and pain.

She would lose Eloise and Jack and they would lose Zac. Zac might be no good in the fidelity stakes but he was already demonstrating sterling traits as a father. And wasn't that why she was supposed to be marrying him?

Practicality rather than sentiment, Zac had re-minded her lethally. A marriage of convenience for both of them, not a marriage based on love or the finer feelings, not even a marriage supposed to last for ever. Her tummy gave a nauseous twist. What had she done? *What had she done?*

She had reacted personally to what she had over-heard in the corridor at the restaurant. She had reacted as if she were marrying for love and had be-haved as though she had been betrayed. Deep down inside herself, she had been bitterly hurt by the idea of other women getting intimate with Zac, imagin-ing them touching him and being touched by him. But was she entitled to such feelings?

On one score, Zac had been correct: they *had* bro-ken up before the ball. Learning that he had had sex with someone else might upset her but he had not betrayed her and he had not broken any promises he made her. Soberly contemplating those facts filled Freddie with chagrin because she had faced Zac in a spirit of angry condemnation.

Yet they weren't in love with each other or even lovers as yet. *Practicality rather than sentiment*, she reflected with an inner shiver of recoil, for, now that she was actually thinking about it, that struck her as a very chilly recipe for a relationship. No wonder Zac had accused her of not taking a realistic view of their marriage. She had reacted emotionally and gone way out of line, driven by her overwhelming need to express her anguished sense of rejection and hurt. But he had neither needed nor wanted such feelings thrown at him. He was not responsible for what she felt, *she* was.

'I had a fight with Zac. The wedding's off as we speak,' she confessed chokily to Claire when she got home.

'Family get-togethers can put people on edge,' Claire remarked with a roll of her eyes. 'Did someone say something that upset you?'

'Something like that,' Freddie mumbled.

'Well, you'd better get round to the hotel and sort it out first thing tomorrow morning with him. If you give the kids breakfast, I'll take over. You have to go for your dress fitting at noon anyway and Richard and I are organised to accompany Zac and the kids to the zoo,' the brunette reminded her drily.

Claire crept into bed, listening to Jack's little snuffles and Eloise's slow peaceful breathing. How could she have forgotten even for a moment what her marrying Zac would mean for the children? Shame dug talon claws of guilt into her tender flesh. She hadn't been willing to have sex with Zac. Was she to blame him for taking what some other woman offered after she had rejected him? Was she really that much of a hypocrite? And why, oh, why had she taken it all so personally when feelings weren't supposed to come into their agreement? She closed her eyes and cringed and wondered if he'd make her grovel and whether she *would* grovel if he made it impossible to do otherwise. It was hardly surprising that she didn't get a wink of sleep that night and was waiting with breakfast on the table before the children even got up.

When she walked into the hotel foyer that morning, Marco immediately approached her. 'The boss expecting you?' he asked.

'Er…no,' Freddie admitted.

'He's in a meeting right now. I'll check.' He spoke in his own language into his headpiece before returning to her side. 'That's fine, Miss Lassiter. Go on up,' he told her, showing her into the lift and putting the card in the slot for her.

Freddie breathed in slow and deep to gather herself. A young woman she didn't recognise opened the penthouse door and ushered her out onto the big balcony where Zac was clearly enjoying a working breakfast while checking over documents with a young dark-haired man. The woman hovered and then sat down beside the man. Zac was back in jeans and a shirt, black hair rippling back from his lean bronzed features, his big powerful body poised in a relaxed sprawl.

'Freddie…meet my personal assistants, Abilio and Catina,' Zac introduced, rising fluidly upright, his eyes a cool luminous pale blue as they always seemed to be in sunlight, roaming over Freddie's stiff little figure with no expression that she could see. If he was surprised at her arrival, he gave no sign of it.

Zac betrayed not an ounce of the relief he'd experienced when he'd heard she was in the hotel. She had worked it all out for herself and he wasn't surprised at that. The night before she had acted on impulse with a temper that was quick to rise but equally quick to subside. Practicality had triumphed. But what would he have done had she not come back? Would he have chased after her? No, he was done with that, he decided decisively. She had to marry him of her own free will, knowing and accepting the limitations of such a marriage. Nothing else would work. But the shadows beneath her eyes, the evidence of a sleepless night troubled him all the same. He was finally beginning to appreciate that nothing about getting married and living with another person was as simple as he wanted to make it.

Freddie shook hands with his companions and then Zac headed indoors, long lithe legs moving at a fast pace. 'We'll take this into the bedroom because we don't want to be interrupted and Abilio and Catina are about to leave.'

'I didn't know you had staff,' Freddie remarked, keen to fill the smouldering silence.

'I may not be running the family empire but I've made a lot of investments on my own behalf with the income,' Zac admitted, lounging back against the solid wooden dresser that sat between the twin windows.

Freddie looked everywhere but at him, her gaze

wandering to the gargantuan bed where the sheets still remained tossed from his occupancy. With a flush she glanced hurriedly away. 'Like this hotel?'

'Exactly.'

Freddie shot him a tense troubled glance. 'I'm here to apologise. I was upset last night. I wasn't thinking things through. I still want to marry you.'

Zac jerked his chin in acknowledgement.

'I was so angry I didn't even think about the children and...what would happen if we split up,' she framed awkwardly.

'Everyone has a price and the children are yours,' Zac drawled softly.

Freddie's eyes flared gold. 'Not *everyone* has a price!' she snapped back at him, nerves taking over and forging past her self-control.

'What else am I supposed to think when you're evidently still prepared to marry an untrustworthy, unreliable womaniser?' he derided silkily.

Put on the spot, Freddie reddened to the roots of her hair. 'I shouldn't have said those things to you. I haven't found you unreliable or untrustworthy and what you chose to do while you were single is none of my business,' she completed with dogged determination. 'But you had better stay faithful to our marriage while I'm still trying to get pregnant because I will *not* share you!'

His lean, strong face darkening, Zac dealt her a brooding appraisal. 'No problem,' he conceded to that condition without argument, because he could not imagine getting bored with her any time soon.

But he did not appreciate that she had only come back because she was terrified of losing the chance to adopt Eloise and Jack. That struck him as ironic when he knew the adoption was the only reason she was marrying him and willing to have a child with him. But something deep and visceral inside him still rebelled against that ego-zapping knowledge.

He studied her slight figure, sheathed in leggings, ankle boots and a jazzy fitted tunic. Her breasts and her hips and a good part of her legs were hidden so he could not understand why just looking at her soft full mouth and caramel-brown eyes made him so aroused. He wondered how long it would take for him to work out the secret of her irresistible attraction, how long it would take for him to get jaded and start living for the day he would get his freedom back. He had never stayed with a woman longer than a week and even then only on the most casual basis. Now, he recognised, he was facing a steep learning curve.

Conscious of Zac's scrutiny and his unsettling silence in the face of her retraction of her insults, Freddie grew increasingly tense, the tip of her tongue sliding out to moisten her dry lips as her breath shortened in her throat. 'So, where do we stand?' she prompted anxiously.

Zac moved forward, seething energy and hunger

powering him. Glittering eyes settled on her tense little face. 'Where we started. Me wanting, you backing away…'

Her breath literally rattled in her throat because without even realising it she had taken a step back as he approached, and in dismay at that awareness she fell still where she stood.

'That's getting old, particularly the day before our wedding.' Zac lifted a lean brown hand to trail a finger along the taut line of her delicate jaw. 'What are you so scared of?'

'I'm not scared,' she told him tightly, but she knew she was lying. Her body was in a state of conflict, her adrenalin buzzing while little internal alarms shrilled inside her. She wanted him close and she wanted to push him away, because pushing men away came more naturally to her than touching one. Yet she *longed* to touch him, to unbutton the shirt stretched across his taut pectoral muscles and trace every rippling leashed line of him with her fingers. She wanted shameless things she had never wanted before and that unnerved her.

Yet the little tingles already ignited by his proximity warred with her alarm system. Her skin prickled, her breasts pushing against the restraint of her bra as her nipples tightened almost painfully. Her mouth ran dry, her breathing rupturing into little snatched spurts of air while her body struggled to combat the wave of heat rising from her pelvis.

'There's nothing to be afraid of,' Zac husked, coiling an arm round her with lazy strength, bending her back to trail a hungry kiss across her delicate collarbone and up the slender column of her neck.

A tiny gasp escaped her, her reactions plunged into overdrive and intensified when he lifted her up against him and then brought her down on the tumbled bed. Eyes flying wide, she gazed up at him in disconcertion and got lost in the blazing magnificence of his crystalline eyes.

'Trust me,' Zac murmured softly, reaching down to flip off her boots and toss them on the floor. 'But at least tell me why you're so scared. Were you assaulted? *Hurt?*'

'No…*no*.' Freddie tried and failed to swallow, fighting to gather her wits. 'But, you know, I saw things…when I was living with my sister…and it put me off…er…sex,' she mumbled as he embarked on her leggings, tugging them down to expose her legs.

'Anything you don't like, you only have to tell me,' Zac told her thickly. 'Any time you want me to stop, I will.'

'O-Okay,' she stammered, barely grasping how she had arrived on the bed and wondering if she should be moving away, reminding him that he had agreed to wait until they were married. Only that restriction seemed so petty now in retrospect that she couldn't make herself voice that reminder. Tomorrow they would be married and all such restraint would naturally be at an end.

Her leggings went flying and she gulped, feeling overpowered and out of her depth with her rather shabby cheap knickers on view. And she was with a guy who loved luxury lingerie, she recalled in intense mortification, yanking her tunic down to cover herself again.

'*Fique tranquilo*…don't worry,' Zac urged, convinced she was ready to flee at any moment. 'I'm worrying enough for both of us.'

Taken aback, Freddie gazed up at him in astonishment. 'What do you have to worry about?'

A flashing grin softened the taut line of Zac's mobile mouth. 'I've never been with a virgin before. I want to make it good for you but I don't know if that's possible.'

'Kiss me,' she heard herself say.

He pressed a soft kiss to her lips and she stopped breathing, her heart hammering a frenzied beat.

'Once more…with enthusiasm,' Freddie whispered uncertainly.

And Zac laughed and covered her mouth again with his to extract a forceful, demanding kiss. He nipped at her lips, stroked her tongue, flicked the roof of her mouth and she started trembling, liquid heat rising from the heart of her.

He lifted his head and, gathering her tunic in his hands, he lifted it up and off her. She crossed her arms over her bra. 'I'm not very big,' she warned him apologetically.

He released the catch at her slender spine and she bowed forward as if to hide herself from him but he pressed her back against the pillows as he whisked the garment away. Her hands fell away because she felt foolish trying to conceal her body from the man she was about to marry. She closed her eyes tightly, fearful of seeing disappointment in his gaze when he realised that she wore a padded bra and was in truth more fried egg than full English breakfast.

'You have very pretty breasts,' Zac husked appreciatively, scanning the pert swell of her dainty curves and the pale delicate pink nipples adorning them.

'You forgot to say little,' she muttered awkwardly.

'Not the first thing that comes to mind,' Zac confided, lowering his dark head to apply his mouth to a quivering pink bud and lash it hungrily with his tongue.

Freddie jerked, her hips rising involuntarily, her whole awareness suddenly centred solely on what he was doing to her. Long skilled fingers skated a pattern over the stretched-tight fabric between her legs and she held her breath as he freed her of that final barrier. She shivered as he explored her with gentle fingers, stroking, teasingly probing, setting off screaming nerve endings and tingles wherever he dallied. She hadn't known she would be so sensitive that the gathering tide of pleasure would almost hurt with its intensity, and then he was rising over her and peeling off his shirt.

Nervous tension tugged at her because he was so much bigger and stronger than she was, his biceps bulging, his splendid torso a masculine vision of sleek bronzed and inked skin stretched over a solid wall of muscle. He rolled off the bed to remove his jeans, peeling them down, exposing the intimidating bulge at his groin outlined by his boxers. Then the boxers went and his long, hard length jutted out, clearly primed and ready for action, and she gulped, wondering how he was planning to fit *that* inside her without hurting her.

Freddie lay rigid, assuming they were in the final phase of intimacy and that it would all be over soon. Zac came back to her and kissed her with a devastating off-the-charts hunger, his tongue delving and teasing, mimicking a far more basic action. Her body softened in the momentary hard embrace of his and then he was sliding down over her, toying with her on the way, a tongue flicking a straining nipple, a kiss bestowed on her belly button, his hands closing over her thighs to part them.

'What are you doing?' she gasped when he kept on moving.

'Trust me,' Zac urged thickly. 'You can't have sex without foreplay. The more ready you are, the less it will hurt.'

Shut up, shut up, she told herself in feverish embarrassment. After all, he knew stuff she didn't. There had been nothing delicate or seductive about the sleazy encounters she had unwillingly witnessed when she was young and impressionable. She shut her eyes tight, surrendering control, banishing the images that had frightened her off sexual experimentation. Contrary to her expectations, Zac was being neither rough nor crude.

His tongue swiped over her and her hips lifted off the mattress in response. Nothing had ever felt so shockingly good and the ache deep inside her intensified its grip. Her legs trembled in his hold as he continued and the building tide of warmth and excitement made her shake. A bone-deep hunger was coalescing at the heart of her and surging higher and higher until at last she reached the pinnacle and the world exploded in glorious colour, leaving her quaking and breathless, absolutely wrecked by the intensity of her first orgasm.

'You are very, very sexy,' Zac growled as he came over her, all virile power and strength, his eyes luminous in the sunlight falling over the bed. 'But we have to go slow now…'

Freddie wasn't quite sure what planet she was on at that moment or what they were to go slowly with but that mental blankness evaporated as he spread her wide and sank into her, slowly stretching her with his fullness. A pinch of discomfort made her grimace and he froze.

'Don't move,' he told her raggedly, his big powerful body arrested over hers as he struggled to resist his need to plunge deep and hard.

Wide-eyed, she stared up at him, her face hectically flushed as he pulled back from her and then shifted forward to sink deep. A hot slice of pain pierced her for an instant and then faded away again.

'Think that's the worst over,' she mumbled.

'And now for the best,' Zac grated, circling his hips to stretch her with a hungry groan about how tight she was and then moving with a fluid rhythm that her body seemed to know as if it had been born for it.

There was no more pain, only gathering passion and increased sensation. She arched up in response as he plunged deeper with every thrust, sending pulsing, voluptuous waves of pleasure surging through her laced with mounting excitement. Her heart pounded so loudly she thought she could hear it and the edgy building tension in her pelvis was rising again until she couldn't hold it back any more and she reached another climax. He thrust into her weak, unresisting body one final time and then stilled with a deep masculine growl of satisfaction.

By the time that Freddie registered that the main act was over, Zac was already out of the bed and striding towards the bathroom. 'Do you want a bath?' he called over a muscular brown shoulder.

Freddie watched his bare bronzed body disappear from view, the intimacy strangely shocking even after what they had just shared.

'Do you?' Zac prompted.

'Yes.' Finally recalling the question and registering that it was broad daylight, she retrieved her brain, but still could not help feeling that it would have been lovely if Zac had held her close for a while after the sex.

But that was being silly, wasn't it? Practicality, not sentiment, she reminded herself in reproof, fearful of attaching any deeper significance to what they had shared. Sex didn't mean anything special to Zac, she told herself firmly. It was nothing more to him than a brief physical release. He had given her pleasure and she should be grateful for that and expect nothing more complex.

Yet insecurity still dogged Freddie. Having gathered up her discarded clothing, she crept into the bathroom and snatched a towel off the rail to wrap it round her.

'Umm...' She fumbled as Zac straightened. 'Was it OK for you?'

Zac shot her a heart-stopping smile of surprise and laughed, his darkly handsome lean features compelling. 'It was wonderful and now you can stop worrying about it.'

'I wasn't worrying... *Zac*!' she yelped in disconcertion as he twitched her out of the towel's folds and lifted her to settle her down into the bath he had run for her. She was taken aback by how natural it felt to be with him in such circumstances while the tender ache between her thighs reminded her of how physically close they had been. Physically close, *not* mentally close, she conceded ruefully.

'I hope you don't get pregnant *too* quickly, *meu pequenino*,' Zac confided, running his bright silvery eyes over her flushed and beautiful face. 'I'm looking forward to having a lot of fun with you in the short term.'

Sex as a simple fun activity was beyond Freddie's imagination but she could see that it was very much Zac's approach and that daunted her. He strode into the shower, evidently in the best of moods, and to console herself she counted her blessings. The sex had been acceptable, their wedding was still on and the adoption application was progressing.

Short term, he had been careful to remind her, she mused, her shoulders drooping a little. Fun in the short term. Could she do that? She *had* to do it. Too much would be lost if she failed to maintain a good relationship with Zac. She had to at least try to do things his way even if it felt foreign and threatening to embrace such beliefs. Only if they were reasonably content as a couple would the children thrive.

In the shower, Zac was weighing up the use of

birth control against his legal need for a child and marvelling at the unexpected direction his thoughts were wandering in. Freddie could conceive immediately, which would kill the fun angle because he knew from his mother's experience that pregnant women got sick, tired and hormonal. If he used condoms, however, they could enjoy carefree sex for as long as they liked. He was already wondering how soon he could enjoy her again. He couldn't wait to see that dreamy, dizzy expression of bliss on her face again and revel in her honest, innocent openness because he had never had that connection with a woman before.

Freddie was a rare find, he conceded with satisfaction. Should he have told her the truth about that night at the ball? He grimaced. He didn't believe in baring his soul and he didn't want to risk hurting her. If he told her the truth she would misinterpret it and make feminine assumptions that would not fit the frame. Wouldn't she assume that she meant more to him than she did? He didn't want to do that to her. Inevitably what he felt would wear off and he would want other women and the freedom to enjoy them anywhere, any place, any time. He knew his own flaws. He was not a for-ever kind of guy and there was a limit to how honest he could afford to be.

CHAPTER SEVEN

IT WAS A breathtaking dress, Freddie reflected, dizzily studying her appearance in the mirror in Claire's bedroom. Getting ready in her own room had proved impossible because there simply wasn't enough space.

The sleek handmade lace bodice with a low back clung from shoulder to hip, playing up her small curves and making her look taller. The skirt fell in intricate cobweb-fine lace folds shimmering with beadwork. At her throat glittered a diamond pendant, a wedding gift from Zac. Her hair was up in an elaborate coronet to support the diamond-studded tiara that Zac had told her had belonged to his late mother, along with the diamond earrings and bracelet she wore.

'Do I look like a Christmas tree?' she asked her aunt worriedly.

'Like I should have that problem!' Claire quipped enviously. 'But diamonds are the family business, so I suppose you have to put the finest on display. Your life will be *so* different, Freddie. It'll be champagne and caviar all the way now.'

Freddie swallowed hard at the thought because she still couldn't imagine it. A hair stylist and a beautician might have come to the house to prepare her for the wedding, but that had seemed more of a necessity than a luxury when she was marrying Zac and she needed to look like the sort of woman that he would marry. Heaven forbid that he would ever look at her and feel embarrassed by her and, thanks to that family dinner, she already knew that even those closest to him could be both critical and judgemental.

Zac, waiting at the church, forced a polite smile when Vitale came to join his two brothers. 'Your majesty,' he said, acknowledging that his half-brother had become the King of Lerovia since his mother's abdication even though the formal coronation would not be held for several months. 'I should be bowing, right?'

'No...not within the family,' King Vitale declared. 'And I intend to have a modern court, so there'll be a lot less bowing and scraping in Lerovia as well. By the way, our wedding present, which is car-shaped, is on its way back to you.'

Zac frowned at that reference to the prized sports car he had lost in that ill-judged bet with his half-brother. '*Back* to me?'

Vitale shrugged. 'Nobody won that bet. You may

not have brought Freddie to the royal ball but now you're *marrying* her—'

'You won fair and square,' Zac began inflexibly.

Angel frowned with the air of a man who would have liked to knock both his stiff-necked brothers' heads together. 'He'll be delighted to accept his car back.'

With a stark exhalation of breath, Zac accepted that loaded hint and murmured through gritted teeth, 'That's very generous of you, Vitale…thanks.'

'And within the family circle there will be neither bows *nor* any more bets,' Angel suggested with quiet emphasis.

Zac sank back into brooding silence, disturbed that he was so tense. People got married every day, he reminded himself. *He* didn't, though, and the surroundings and the stifling traditions made him feel constrained. The whole event was much more formal than he had expected.

The bride made quite a picture walking down the aisle with Jack, loveable with his hair in corn rows and clad in a miniature suit toddling along beside her and Claire. Eloise was walking very carefully behind her aunts clutching a basket of flowers and clad in the pink flouncy princess dress that was the summit of her little-girl dreams. Zac discovered that he couldn't take his eyes off that little tableau. His family, his *new* family, he realised suddenly as Jack beamed trustingly at him and Eloise waved from behind her aunts as if afraid that he might not notice her.

Without the smallest warning, the enormity of the responsibility he had taken on engulfed Zac. He tried to concentrate his attention on Freddie, who looked stunning, sexy and cute as hell, but all the while his brain was running at a mile a minute, telling him that freedom of any kind would be an unattainable luxury with one woman and two…eventually *three*… children depending on him to be a good husband and a good father. He lost colour, his spectacular bone structure tautly delineated below his bronzed skin as the ramifications of such a marriage finally sank in on him: he would *never* be totally free again because parenting was *for ever*, with no get-out clause. It was a sobering moment, most particularly when he was willing to admit that he didn't know the first thing about how to take care of anyone but himself.

Freddie's hands almost crushed her bouquet of white and pink roses when she glimpsed the cool bleak light forming in Zac's gorgeous eyes and the absence of his trademark grin. Her heart sank like a stone. He was disappointed in her. Did she not look the way he had imagined she would? Had he believed a designer dress and all the trimmings, not to mention the family diamonds, would transform an ordinary waitress into something rather more special? Or did he have cold feet about getting married? Whatever it was, he did not look happy, which he should have been, considering that their marriage was supposed to provide what he most wanted as well.

A child. *Their* first child to add to the mix of Eloise and Jack, whom Zac had insisted must share their day with them because he wanted them to have that first memory of the four of them becoming a family. Zac had never had that family experience, although Freddie had happily enjoyed it for the first ten years of her life. Zac, however, had known only rejection from those who should have given him love and support. By the time he got to know his real father, who *was* a caring man, it had been a case of too little too late. Of course, Zac was damaged by such a loveless childhood but wasn't it her role to ensure that he realised that together they could make things different for their own children? Or was that too tall an order for a new bride, who wasn't loved, to take on? She was rather afraid that it might be…

Her anxiety about Zac shielded her from the pressure of the church packed with rich, smartly dressed guests. Zac had many business acquaintances and his father, still keen to show off his newly discovered son, had invited his friends to share their day as well. His brothers were attending with small parties, further pushing up the numbers. Freddie, however, had only had a few friends to invite because her social life had been very much curtailed by the children.

The priest welcomed them to the altar and gave a serious opening speech about the responsibilities of marriage. When she reached for Zac's hand, it was ice cool in hers. She had a sudden disturbing and panic-inducing vision of him walking out on her at the last possible minute and, instinctively, she held on tight. The ceremony began and Jack escaped Claire to cling to Zac's knees like a limpet and loudly wail in disappointment when someone lifted him away. Zac raised Freddie's hand and slid the twisted platinum ring onto her wedding finger.

They had picked it together but there hadn't been much choice because her extravagant engagement ring took up so much space that there was little left to spare for the wedding ring she would wear. Zac had laughed heartily at the time, teasing her about her little hands and short fingers, and without warning tears stung her eyes at that memory. He had been so laid-back and light-hearted that day only a week earlier and his current change of mood unnerved her. He had wanted to marry her, *he* had asked *her* to marry him, she reminded herself to bolster her spirits.

They signed the register with his brother and Claire as witnesses and by the time they walked down the aisle at speed it was obvious that Zac could not wait to get out of the church.

On the steps, as the guests held up phones to photograph them, he expelled his breath in a hiss. '*Meu Deus*…glad that's over!'

Eloise clung to the foot of his jacket and Jack held out his arms, almost toppling out of Claire's hold.

'Tough, isn't it, Jack?' Zac derided, reaching out to take the over-eager baby into his arms, recognising that his shenanigans had taxed Claire's low patience threshold.

It was a challenge for Freddie to hold onto her bridal beam in Zac's radius, particularly after she saw Angel and Vitale exchanging meaningful looks across the disenchanted bridegroom. Getting into the limousine even with the children clambering over them was a relief because at least there were no watching eyes and listening ears there.

'What's wrong, Zac?' Freddie asked levelly.

'Nothing's wrong,' Zac intoned. 'I'm just not cut out for this kind of stuff.'

'You insisted on this being what you called a *normal* wedding,' she reminded him.

His strong jaw line clenched and his wide sensual mouth compressed, his crystalline eyes sombre below his semi-lowered lashes. 'We all make mistakes,' he said very drily, thinking that he should have opted to avoid the traditional hoopla and travel a simpler route.

Freddie froze. *'Am I a mistake?'* she suddenly demanded loudly.

Zac groaned long and low. 'You know I didn't mean it like that...*inferno*, I don't know what I meant! But that priest lecturing us on our marital duties reminded me of being at school,' he bit out impatiently.

Freddie embraced silence all the way to The Palm Tree, where the reception was being staged. Zac had dispensed with a greeting line as being too official and instead the guests mingled over drinks when they arrived. The hotel nanny was at their disposal and the children were borne off for lunch and a nap. Zac vanished into the bar before they sat down to their meal, reappearing just in time to make a very short speech in the wake of his father's. He ate little and drank a lot, responding to Freddie when she spoke but initiating no other conversation. He seemed bleakly set on just going through the motions and getting through what he clearly saw as an ordeal.

Somehow it infuriated Freddie that, even in a mood, Zac should still look utterly gorgeous, dark stubble beginning to shade in the angles and hollows of his beautiful bone structure, black lashes low over his brooding glittering gaze as he lounged back with careless elegance in his seat.

Exasperated by her susceptibility to him, Freddie tore her attention from him and went into the cloakroom to freshen up. She was grimacing at her downcast expression when a woman appeared in the mirror beside her.

'I hope Zac treats you better than he treated my daughter,' she remarked curtly.

Blinking, Freddie turned her head to look at the ageing blonde, studying her with pursed lips. 'Sorry?' she said blankly.

'Two years ago my daughter was working as a chalet girl in Klosters. Zac told her that she was the most beautiful girl in the world...well, actually she *was* a runner-up in the Miss World competition the year before,' the woman digressed with pride. 'Anyway. She was with him a week and then she never heard from him again. He broke her heart.'

Freddie straightened her slight shoulders and lifted her chin. 'And you're telling me this because...?'

'He loses interest once the chase is over. I thought I should warn you.'

'Thank you,' Freddie replied with equal insincerity, laced with a tight determined smile as she walked away.

Merry greeted her when she returned to their table to find Zac's chair empty.

'He's doing shots in the bar with Angel,' Angel's wife confided with a visible wince of embarrassment.

The guests were waiting for the bride and groom to open the dancing. Freddie persuaded the new King and Queen of Lerovia to do the honours instead and cut the cake with her new father-in-law's help because she was resolutely set on not chasing after Zac to nag at him to do anything he didn't want to do. Feeling suitably martyred, she sat with Merry and Jazz and got to know the two other women better while little Elyssa, Merry's daughter, played at their feet and Jazz shared the news that she was expecting twins, although her willowy frame showed little evidence of that reality.

Freddie and Zac were scheduled to leave the hotel at five and as soon as the kids had had an early supper Freddie went up to the penthouse to get changed. She put on silky wide-legged trousers and a floaty top for their flight to the South of France and only then went off to locate her new husband.

'Zac's waiting in the limo. His bodyguards took him out the back entrance,' Angel told her warily. 'He's drunk. Blame me.'

'Oh, I'm not blaming anyone!' Freddie said a tinge shrilly, her face as hot as hellfire.

'I think…' Charles Russell interposed anxiously, 'Zac was celebrating too hard.'

Freddie raised both brows, feeling like the original toxic bride with everyone trying to placate her. 'I don't think he was celebrating getting married. I think he was drowning his sorrows.'

'Zac can be a little unpredictable,' Angel volunteered, contriving to look both guilty and sympathetic. 'And he doesn't normally drink this much.'

Freddie shone a bright smile at their anxious faces, her pride badly stung by his family's concern on her behalf. And just behind that lurked her depressing recollection of the woman who had accosted her in the cloakroom to tell her that Zac lost interest in a woman once the chase was over. Since his dogged pursuit of her had ended in his penthouse bedroom the day before, she reckoned that there could be some truth in that disturbing allegation. Now that he had discovered that she was just like every other woman he had slept with, he evidently didn't even have enough interest left to stay sober for their wedding night, she thought with a mixture of anger, hurt and exasperation.

After all, as one of the former bar staff, she knew rather more than Zac's family did about his drinking habits, she reflected ruefully. Zac usually drank more coffee than alcohol, so if he had drunk a lot it could only be because something had upset him. And considering this was their wedding day, what else was she to blame for his mood than their new marriage?

Freddie didn't speak a word on the drive to the airport but Zac was too preoccupied to notice. He followed his bodyguards out of the car while she hung back with the children and they were rushed through VIP channels out to the da Rocha private jet. Zac boarded, sent her a careless glance and murmured, 'I'm going to lie down for a while.' And off he went, leaving Freddie to deal with Isabel, the young smiling nanny, waiting to help her with the children, the nanny Zac hadn't even thought to mention he had engaged.

Mercifully it was a large jet and there was a second sleeping compartment already prepared for the children's occupancy. Jack was already asleep but Eloise was very reluctant to go to bed at the same time as her little brother, and the nanny entertained her at the rear of the main cabin while Freddie took the time to eat a light evening meal and flip through the glossy magazines provided for her. She was absolutely enraged with Zac and holding it in was like trying to contain a screeching storm.

Zac emerged shortly before they landed and lifted Eloise, who, like Jack, was fast asleep. They would have been wiser to stay in London the first night and travel by day, Freddie acknowledged ruefully, but Zac had not consulted her. Having landed, they transferred to a helicopter, which took off with a lurch that sent Freddie's stomach plummeting. The racket of the rotors woke Jack up and he burst into frightened sobs. Finding himself with a stranger, he was inconsolable and Freddie reclaimed him with relief as soon as the helicopter landed again.

A weathered stone building loomed ahead of them, every tall window brilliantly lit up in welcome. Zac removed Jack from Freddie's arms. 'I'll take him. You look exhausted.'

Zac had returned to planet earth again, she registered irritably, feeling that she could have done without being told that she looked so tired. She wasn't vain but she had lived through a disastrous wedding day polished up to her very best and had received not a single compliment from her uninterested bridegroom. She said nothing as they trudged up the path towards the brightly lit frontage of the massive house.

The house reminded her of a postcard of a fantasy Provencal retreat, replete as it was with regimented lines of painted smoky blue shutters and flowers and terracotta vases ornamenting every window and door. But even with the light fading fast she could see the bulk of the house stretching back, recognising that it far outstripped in size any normal house. The number of staff waiting to greet them in the marble-floored hall was another reminder that she had married a man who was unaccustomed to looking after himself in any way. He handed Jack straight over to a young woman. 'This is Jennifer, Freddie. She will be helping Isabel with the kids.'

Jack screeched at physical contact with yet another stranger and almost threw himself out of the unfortunate Jennifer's arms. Freddie grabbed him back. 'It's all right. I'll see to settling the children down tonight. They're overtired and nervous of strangers,' she said apologetically.

Jennifer showed the way upstairs to the rooms readied for the children and Freddie heaved a sigh of relief at the freedom to do something familiar even if it was in an unfamiliar place. *Two* nannies? Was he crazy? Was he expecting Eloise and Jack to be kept out of sight by staff as children had been for centuries in well-off families? Who did he think he was to make such arrangements without involving her?

She wanted to strangle Zac and scream at him and it was an effort to smile gratefully at the nannies as she sat down to rock Jack back to sleep in what was undoubtedly the nursery of a little boy's dreams, with a cot shaped like a race car. By the time she got Jack ensconced in his cot and went into the bedroom next door, Eloise was already sleeping peacefully in a miniature four-poster bed draped in pink. All the luxury surrounding her, all the fancy toys piled up waiting to be played with, felt surreal and foreign and alienating to Freddie, and for a moment she wanted desperately to be back in the safe confines of the tiny bedroom she had shared with her niece and nephew.

Instead she had a housekeeper introducing herself as Mariette in broken English and offering to show her to the master bedroom suite. Once again, Zac was nowhere to be seen and at that moment, feeling totally isolated, Freddie didn't care. She wanted normal and for her that meant a shower and a bed and the renewed strength that would come from a good night's sleep. She had barely slept at all the previous night, lying awake dreamily thinking about Zac, her first sexual experience and their future together. Now the chances of them achieving some rosy perfect state of coupledom struck her as both pathetic and unlikely.

Zac walked into the master suite at one in the morning, the need to make amends having finally overcome his fierce pride, but he was too late. Freddie was already dead to the world, curled up in a tight little ball hugging a pillow on the far side of the bed. He studied her, the flush of sleep on her delicate features, the tousled dark blonde hair playing across the pillow, the relaxed line of her lush pink mouth. So lovely and so fragile, he acknowledged reluctantly, and he had hurt her. Getting married was fast proving to be a learning experience and the first lesson was that his behaviour affected her as well. Pretty basic one that, he acknowledged grimly, but then Zac had never had another person's needs and wishes to consider before.

In the morning, he would make everything right, he assured himself. Quite how to go about achieving that objective escaped him, but he was fairly sure that some serious thought would give him the answer. But why the hell had he brought her to the Villa Antonella, a place haunted by his earliest bad memories? The place where his short-lived but once normal family life had disintegrated into messy broken shards overnight?

He couldn't answer that question either.

CHAPTER EIGHT

FEELING ALMOST REJUVENATED by a night of unbroken rest, Freddie bounced out of bed and then looked at the time and almost laid an egg. What about the children? She should have been up two hours earlier to look after them! And then she remembered the nannies and the guilt ebbed, but only very slowly because feeding Eloise and Jack still felt like *her* job.

After another shower, she applied the lightest possible make-up from the new stash that had been part of her makeover and selected a cool cotton sundress from the new wardrobe of summer clothing Zac had ordered on her behalf. Only then did she feel ready to greet the sunshine blazing through the tall windows.

Zac was always *giving* her stuff. He was very generous, she acknowledged ruefully, but it didn't cancel out his stubborn go-it-alone attitude. She headed to the children's bedrooms first but both were empty. Jennifer was coming upstairs as Freddie went down and informed her that Eloise and Jack were with Zac out on the terrace. She was disconcerted by that news, for she had uncharitably assumed that the hiring of *two* nannies indicated that Zac wanted the kids kept out of his hair as much as possible. Mariette showed her out to the wide stone terrace that ran along the rear of the house to take advantage of the truly spectacular panoramic view across the rural valley behind it.

Freddie came to a sudden halt to appreciate the landscape. Olive trees with silvery foliage crowded terraces ringed by ancient stone walls and lavender fields stretched over the furthest hill, the brilliant purple furrows of blooms seeming to perfume the fresh air. The terrace was shaded by an ornate ironwork pergola lushly wrapped in grape vines and wisteria.

'Auntie Freddie... Auntie Freddie!' Eloise came running down the terrace to show her a picture of a dragon, or was it two dragons? 'See...they getting married.'

'Very nice,' Freddie assured her niece, trying not to notice that the larger dragon shape was adorned with what looked very like a tattoo. Eloise was already demonstrating a natural artistic ability that far outstripped her age group.

Tension laced Freddie's slight frame when she saw Zac rising from the table at the far end while Jack literally tried to run to her.

As she hastily scooped up Jack before he fell, for

while he could walk he could not yet run, she noticed
that Zac had forsaken his business suits in favour
of close-fitting jeans and a white linen shirt against
which his skin glowed. He looked, Freddie thought
resentfully, like a health advert, not at all like a man
who should've been nursing a monster hangover. She
moved towards him stiffly, face tight, eyes evasive
as she set Jack down to play with the toys scattered
across the terrace.

'Mariette is bringing your breakfast,' Zac murmured casually.

'I didn't ask for any.'

'I ordered for you.'

'But you don't know what I wanted,' Freddie
pointed out thinly.

'I ordered a selection,' Zac assured her with a
steely glint in his brilliant eyes as he surveyed her.
'You suit blue. You look lovely.'

'I seriously doubt that,' Freddie countered with an
angry flush, thinking of how her perfectly groomed
self the day before had failed to attract such interest.

'Let's not argue in front of the kids,' Zac urged
warningly.

Resenting that reproof, Freddie breathed in so
deep that she was vaguely surprised she didn't ex-
plode like a bag of hot air, because suddenly she was
so angry with him that she could barely breathe and
hold the furious words in.

'These are for you…' Zac announced, lifting an

elaborate and very large bouquet of flowers in a vase up onto the table. 'And this…'

'*This*' was a jewellery box, and she didn't want to open it. Flowers, and presumably diamonds. He had utilised a whole host of brain cells to come up with those as an apology, she thought nastily, but neither gift hit the right spot. She glanced at him, reading the wary light in his glorious crystalline eyes, the wariness of a man dealing with an unknown quantity and wondering how she would react.

Mariette arrived with an entire trolley of food and a maid to serve. Freddie felt embarrassed accepting only fruit, a croissant and a cup of tea. But even the melting tenderness of the pastry fought to make it past her tight throat. Did she give Zac the benefit of the doubt and move on past the debacle of their wedding day? Even if she didn't feel the smallest bit forgiving? As a rule she didn't sulk or hold spite, but he *had* to explain himself at the very least, she decided. She lifted the jewellery box so that he couldn't call her bad mannered and flipped up the lid on a diamond-studded gold watch.

'Wow…thank you so much,' she said generously, determined to be gracious, glancing across at him. Momentarily those lean, darkly handsome features surrounded by his blue-black luxuriant hair and accentuated by those bright pale blue eyes literally blew her concentration to smithereens.

'How can you drink tea instead of coffee in the

morning?' Zac asked inconsequentially, watching her with an intensity that made her skin tighten over her bones and set up a disturbing throb between her thighs.

'It's what I'm used to,' she muttered, recognising that he planned to gloss over the whole wedding day thing without even making an actual apology aside of the flowers and the watch, and recognising too that she could never look herself in the face again if she allowed him to use his electrifying sexuality to derail her.

Jennifer and Isabel arrived to collect the children to take them out into the garden. An unearthly silence fell across the terrace after their departure and Freddie swallowed hard, still picking nervously at shreds of her croissant.

Entranced, Zac watched her pluck another shred of pastry and place it between her moist pink lips and his jeans tightened. He thought about sex. She clasped the watch round her slender wrist. He thought about more sex. He discounted her tension, reckoning that what they both needed was a good rousing tumble in bed to find each other again.

'Are you planning to say sorry?' Freddie asked, shattering both his expectations and his mood. 'Even *thinking* about it? Or is it just a case of not being able to get the words out?'

'You know that I regret my attitude yesterday,' Zac told her tautly. 'It's obvious, isn't it?'

Freddie nodded. 'But you can't expect flowers and a designer watch to do the job for you.'

'They always have in the past.'

'Then you've been mixing with the wrong kind of woman,' Freddie responded acidly. 'And to be frank, sorry wouldn't even begin to cover it.'

Zac sprang out of his chair, the legs of it scraping harshly across the stone tiles beneath. 'I got drunk. I didn't kill anyone!' he flashed back at her with sudden anger.

'You pretty much opted out of our entire wedding day,' Freddie declared, shaken by that anger but persisting. 'You weren't there to start the dancing with me. You weren't there even to cut the cake. It was humiliating and hurtful and, obviously, people noticed your absence. All I need you to do now is explain *why*...'

'I'm no good at those kinds of explanations.'

'But you could, at least, *try*,' Freddie said gently.

'*Meu Deus*...what do you want from me?' Zac demanded rawly. 'An apology? You already have it.'

'I need to know why—'

'No, you don't!' Zac fired back at her, his broad chest heaving as he dragged in a deep sustaining breath. 'You *don't*. I don't have that kind of conversation with women.'

'I'll forgive and forget if you just tell me why,' Freddie exclaimed in appeal. 'I need to understand.'

Rage glittering in his glorious eyes and the sense

of being trapped intensifying, Zac compressed his lips hard. 'I won't argue with you. I'm going out for a while,' he told her, turning on his heel and striding down the terrace at speed.

For a startled moment, Freddie simply stared after him and then she chased after him, only to be greeted by the slam of the front door and a look of curious enquiry from Mariette. Her face colouring, she returned to the terrace, now blind to the wonderful view. He had walked out sooner than talk—not a very productive approach to a new marriage. But was she expecting too much from him too soon? Their marriage was not supposed to be a meeting of hearts and minds.

Practicality not sentiment.

The words rang like a falling tombstone of foreboding at the back of her mind.

Zac backed away from conflict, reluctant to get that involved with anyone. She couldn't live like that, she thought fearfully, never really knowing where she stood with him. But he had told her where she stood before they married, hadn't he? Practicality covered everything and emotions didn't have to be considered. But what if she already felt more than she should for him? Freddie grimaced at that suspicion but there it was, feelings she couldn't avoid, feelings he wouldn't want her to feel. It hurt when he walked away, refusing to answer her questions, refusing to shed a glimmer of light on what went on in that complex head of his, because hopefully if she understood better she could forgive more easily. Tears prickled her eyes as she sat there and listened to the roar of a powerful motorbike firing up and then the quieter sound of his security team following in a car.

Was she so unreasonable? Had she driven him away? And when would he return?

Zac travelled quite a distance before he cooled off. Angel had asked him, if he had the time, to check out the work he was having done on his yacht and report back to him. He drove down to the Saint Laurent du Var Marina and paused at a waterside café to order an espresso, avoiding the glances of a group of youthful tourists giving him inviting looks from nearby. Angel and Vitale seemed to have taken to marriage like ducks to water, Zac reflected resentfully, so why was it all going wrong for him? He had asked Freddie to marry him, had *wanted* her to marry him. He had chosen her and would still have chosen her even when she was almost shouting at him, he acknowledged grudgingly. But she wanted more from him than any other woman ever had. The flowers and the watch hadn't cut the ice.

What had come over him at the wedding? He was accustomed to responsibility but not to being responsible for other people, with the exception of employees with whom he had no personal ties. From childhood he had learned to hold people at bay to ensure they couldn't hurt him. If he didn't let anyone get close he was safe. But Freddie and the children weren't going to hurt or betray him. He was more likely to hurt them by failing to live up to their expectations, he reasoned impatiently. What if she fell in love with him? He would have to warn her off on that score. The very last thing he wanted to do was hurt Freddie, he acknowledged without hesitation. Or Eloise, or Jack. He was getting attached to the three of them even if he wasn't supposed to do so.

Practicality not sentiment, he reminded himself with a groan of frustration. But practicality didn't take any account of emotions or emotional women. And Freddie was emotional, all wide, accusing, hurt eyes and quivering lips. Eloise looked at him in much the same way when he refused to read the dragon story twice over at the same sitting. Jack? Jack was simple in his demands, content solely with attention.

Freddie's emotional outlook, however, was infinitely preferable to the kind of brassy, avaricious females who littered his past, Zac conceded wryly. She stood up for herself too. She wasn't a doormat eager to agree with everything he did and said. Freddie hadn't wanted the watch, she had wanted words, only what was he to do when the words wouldn't be the ones she wanted to hear? Honesty at any cost? What woman really wanted that?

* * *

The day went past very slowly for Freddie because Zac was such an unknown quantity. For all she knew he could have flown back to London or Brazil or even gone off with another, less demanding woman. 'Unpredictable', Angel Valtinos had labelled his half-brother, and now for the first time she was seeing that in Zac and it unnerved her that a simple request for an explanation could infuriate him to such an extent. She bathed the children and saw them into bed, promising that Zac would be back soon and praying that she was right.

She was shocked when she walked out onto the terrace and saw him simply standing there looking out over the valley.

'Zac…' she breathed with irrefutable relief. 'Where have you been?'

'I went to Nice, checked out the work being done on Angel's yacht…he asked me to,' he told her with a fluid shrug as he slowly turned round to face her. 'How are you?'

'I wasn't sure you'd come back,' she whispered tightly.

'I may storm off but I'll always come back,' Zac murmured with wry amusement. 'I don't like losing my temper with people.'

'I'm not people, I'm your wife,' she protested as the sun went down behind him in a crimson and golden blaze of colour, the light picking up the straight angle of his dark brows above his deep-set eyes and the wide sensual line of his mouth and sending a shiver of awareness travelling through her. 'But I'm not sure you were really ready to take on a wife.'

Zac raked long brown fingers through his black hair and breathed in deep. 'For a split second when I saw you and the children in the church, I felt trapped. I had no excuse to feel like that because I asked you to marry me. Even so, the sudden awareness that I was going to be a husband and a father to two, possibly *three* kids, knocked me sideways. Being free— the ability to get up and go where I like when I like and do as I like—has always been very important to me. The idea of being tied down filled me with—'

'Yes, I get it,' Freddie broke in tightly, ramming down her pain at that honest admission, ironically not wanting him to expand on it. 'It's a massive change for you and maybe you hadn't quite thought it through when you asked me to marry you. But if you want out now, it's *not* too late.'

Zac frowned in bewilderment at that statement. 'It's way too late. What about the adoption?'

Freddie's spine stiffened. 'I would rather give up the children than force you to go through with a marriage you don't want,' she told him starkly, because if they were both unhappy it would only make the children unhappy as well and she owed them a better future than that.

Zac went rigid, every muscle in his lean, powerful body pulling taut. 'That's a crazy offer to make, *meu pequenino*. I wouldn't do that to you.'

'Strictly speaking, we're not fully and legally married yet because we haven't shared a bed. Right now, we could still get an annulment.'

Without warning, Zac was being plunged into a much bigger crisis than he had expected and he wished he had lied about feeling trapped and had skipped the very self-indulgent drinking episode that had followed. 'I don't want an annulment. I don't want to lose you or the children,' he admitted in a driven undertone. 'I behaved badly. You suffered for it. Now I'm thinking more clearly and there is no one else I want to marry, no one else I want to be married to… I can only face sharing those kinds of ties with you,' he completed doggedly.

Freddie finally managed to breathe again. She had believed she *had* to make the offer because she didn't see how she could keep him if he didn't want to be with them. That would be a recipe for disaster. Now, fear and insecurity still pulling at her, she stared up at him anxiously. 'I don't want to make you unhappy.'

'Freddie…in my whole life, nobody ever cared whether or not I was happy!' Zac exclaimed in wonderment. 'Can we go indoors now? Standing right at this spot brings back unfortunate memories of the accident I had here as a child.'

'You came here as a child? And got hurt?'

'Antonella bought this place almost thirty years ago. My mother and stepfather liked to entertain friends here in the summer,' he told her flatly as they traversed the marble foyer. 'I was three and very adventurous. I clambered down the slope and fell and cut my leg badly. Luckily...or unluckily as it later proved...there was a doctor among the friends staying and he saved my life because I had lost a lot of blood.'

Zac had turned pale, his voice roughening as he walked up the imposing staircase. 'They rushed me to hospital, where it transpired that I have a very rare blood group. Charles's blood group. Apparently it had been mentioned at my birth but Afonso didn't pick up on the significance. Afonso believed I was his son and he couldn't understand why he or Antonella couldn't give me blood. His best friend, the doctor, explained that I couldn't possibly be Afonso's child and that's the day my life fell apart as far as family goes.'

Freddie had stopped dead on the stairs to work through what he was telling her. 'Oh, my goodness...' she framed sickly.

'I only remember two things about the whole experience. One was my mother having hysterics for days, the other was Afonso, the man whom I believed to be my father and whom I loved, pushing me away in disgust and calling me a "filthy half-breed",' he concluded heavily. 'Of course, he was upset and furious that he had accepted me as his son.'

Freddie winced and placed a soothing hand on his arm. 'Still no excuse for saying *that* to you. It wasn't your fault.'

'It wasn't anyone's fault. My mother had never admitted to my stepfather that she had had an affair with another man after he broke off their engagement. That was her little secret and she preferred to assume that I was Afonso's child. She went to pieces when the truth came out.'

Freddie's heart was breaking for him. She was imagining how lost and hurt he must have been at only Eloise's age, confronted with such a massive rejection and, indeed, hatred. 'And then what happened?'

'My mother took me back to Brazil and put me on the horse-breeding ranch with servants to look after me. It was over a year before I saw her again. I didn't see Afonso again until last year when he approached me with a business opportunity. I said no.'

'And their marriage survived all that? They stayed together?'

'Afonso enjoyed the da Rocha lifestyle but he was enraged that, as his wife's firstborn, I would inherit rather than any child *he* had with her,' he completed grimly. 'But Antonella refused to accept that reality and she kept on trying to give him a child even after the doctors warned her that she was risking her life. She only finally told me who my father was on the day she died. She was ashamed of it…and of me being illegitimate like she was.'

Freddie struggled to accept that Zac had been punished for his paternity by exclusion and virtual abandonment by his own mother. Simultaneously he had lost the man he'd believed to be his father. In one dreadful day, he had lost his whole family. She remembered how utterly lost she had felt after her parents died and how much she had clung to Lauren for comfort and security. Zac, however, hadn't had the consolation of a sibling.

'I'm surprised you still own this house,' she re-marked as he paused in the ajar doorway of Eloise's bedroom to glance in. Illuminated by the night light she couldn't sleep without, Eloise was a small bump in a sea of cuddly toys. Zac's taut dark features per-ceptibly softened.

'My mother rented it out for years. I don't think she ever came back here and, as social services didn't want us to take the children out of Europe, it made sense for us to use the villa as a base. I was planning to put it on the market when we left. I didn't even realise that I still had memories of this place until I walked through the door,' Zac con-fessed, strolling on to Jack's room and walking in slowly when he saw a little leg dangling out between the cot bars.

Jack was fast asleep in the corner. Freddie leant

down to gently rearrange his warm little body into a more comfortable position.

'He feels like he's mine even though I know he's not,' Zac said softly. 'And it doesn't matter that he's not.'

Freddie's tender smile swept the tension from her triangular face. 'Even people who don't like kids very much warm to Jack's sunny nature.'

'It was very generous of you to offer me an out but I freely choose to stay married to you,' Zac breathed gruffly outside the door. 'Can we start again as if yesterday didn't happen?'

Freddie nodded vigorously, caramel eyes welded to his lean bronzed face, her breathing feathering in her dry throat. His hand closed over hers and the buzz of awareness awakened by that contact sent her every nerve ending into overdrive. A slight quiver ran through her taut frame as they entered the master bedroom she had slept in alone the night before.

'I need a shower.' Zac peeled off his shirt and stripped with the careless ease of a man without a single self-conscious bone in his body.

Freddie watched him walk naked and bronzed into the shower while she removed her make-up and washed her face. He caught her up into his arms while her face was still buried in a towel and she yelped in surprise when he lifted her and carried her back into the bedroom.

'*En quero voce...* I want you,' Zac growled, stand-

ing her up to extract her from her dress and smiling
appreciatively when he discovered that she wore only
knickers beneath.

His hands swept up to capture her breasts, his
thumbs grazing over her sensitive nipples before he
took her mouth with passionate force. Every ratio-
nal thought she had evaporated at the same moment.
Her fingers tightened convulsively on his muscular
shoulders as his aroused body pressed against hers
and excitement sizzled through her as the anxiety of
the day finally melted away.

Zac tumbled her down on the bed and pinned her
beneath him, luminous eyes glinting with amusement below black velvet lashes. 'I wanted to do this
this morning. How would that have gone down?'

'Like a lead balloon,' Freddie framed with difficulty, insanely conscious of the hard pressure of
his arousal against her stomach and even more insanely conscious of the heat and moisture gathering
between her legs.

'Now I want you a hundred times more,' Zac
husked. 'Because you stood up to me.'

'That's weird,' she told him, quivering as the tip
of his tongue traced her delicate collarbone, setting
up unexpected reactions in other places.

'No, it's not. I don't want a yes-woman.'

'You did this morning,' she countered with a grin.

'That's sex, that's different,' he dismissed lazily,
skilled fingers outlining the entrance concealed be-

tween her damp folds, making her tremble and jerk. 'Every guy wants a yes-woman when it comes to sex.'

His honesty made her laugh and he ran teasing fingertips up over her ribcage, discovering where she was ticklish. Freddie made her own exploration over his warm, hard abdominal muscles, fingers straying playfully closer to his bold, hard shaft until frustration forced him to grab her hand and close it round him.

Surprise darted through her at the smooth, hard length of him and she stroked and cupped and shaped and then dropped her head down in an experimental mood, only to be dragged up again.

'I can't take that right now! I need to be inside you,' Zac bit out raggedly as he rearranged her to his satisfaction and plunged into her without ceremony, a guttural sound of satisfaction wrenched from him. '*Voce me excita*…you excite me so much.'

This time there was no discomfort, only the compelling sensation of her body stretching to capacity to accept his. Her hips lifted instinctively in welcome and then he moved and a wave of pulsing excitement was unleashed, her body thrumming like a new engine raring to go. She gasped as his hands cupped her hips to lift her and deepen his penetration.

'You feel like hot satin,' Zac groaned, provocatively withdrawing and then slamming back into her again while her hips squirmed and the heat in her pelvis rose with the tightening, building surge of pressure. 'I thought about this at least once every ten seconds today.'

'Tell me something that surprises me,' Freddie urged, her breath catching in her throat as the hard, virile thrust of his body made her writhe beneath him.

'You do…every time,' Zac groaned, claiming her reddened mouth in a hot, driving kiss.

His heart was thundering against her and she rose up against him one last time, her internal muscles clenching hard as an explosive climax gripped her. Her head fell back against the pillows, her hair in a wild tangle as ripples of melting bliss engulfed her sated length.

Zac reached his own completion with her but bliss seemed to be the last thing on his mind as he reared back from her and swore in Portuguese. *'Inferno…* I forgot to use a condom!' he bit out in exasperation.

'Why would you want to do that?' Freddie asked in dreamy bemusement.

Zac stared down at her, crystalline eyes deadly serious. 'I thought maybe we needed a breathing space to get this marriage up and running and that you might prefer a delay in the baby department.'

'No,' Freddie said decisively. 'Because it could take months and months for me to conceive, so it's easier just to go on as we began. If it happens, it happens.'

Zac released her from his weight and Freddie moved onto her side and draped an arm and a leg across him as he began to move off the bed. 'Where are you going?'

'My room's next door.'

'I thought this was *our* room.'

'I'm used to sleeping alone.'

'Time for a rethink,' Freddie whispered sleepily, fingers toying with his gold necklace of St Jude. 'Why do you wear this?'

'It belonged to my mother. She gave it to me before she died.'

'I want you with me at night,' she admitted.

'Why?' Zac demanded baldly.

'Cosier that way,' his wife mumbled, her arm clamping round him like a chain. 'And if you can shag Miss World chalet girls in Klosters and break their hearts without a blush, you can manage to share a bed with your wife…'

Zac froze and gazed down at her in complete consternation.

'Wasn't going to mention that…it just slipped out.' Freddie sighed regretfully as she snuggled up against him, impervious to all loaded hints.

'I don't want to break your heart,' Zac told her levelly, rather than demanding to know her source.

Freddie opened her eyes and looked languorously up at him. 'I don't fall for players, so you're safe. Anyway, my heart's fully wrapped up in the children.'

'*Que bom*…that's good,' Zac assured her, wondering why he should almost feel affronted by that comforting assurance. 'Love's a complication we definitely don't need when we're not staying together.'

Not staying together.

That reminder rocked through Freddie like an earthquake and sliced into her heart. Too proud to show any reaction, she fell still, instructing herself firmly to go to sleep. She had got too comfortable with him for a moment and had forgotten about the limits of their relationship. Perhaps she shouldn't have asked him to share the bed with her. Now she had plunged them into an intimacy that he had plainly told her was inappropriate. Of course, it was, she told herself uncomfortably. Their marriage was a sham because it was temporary and she had agreed to that condition, hadn't she?

Zac let most of his tension bleed out of him again. The innate urge to push her away had receded. She wasn't doing him any harm. She was just overly affectionate, which was a good trait for a mother of three to have, he conceded reflectively. He could share the bed, of course he could, but he still believed it would have been wiser to keep some constraint between them. After all, what they had wasn't permanent and the less they shared now, the easier it would be to part.

On the other hand, he could wake her up slowly

in a few hours and revel in the benefits of sharing space, he thought with reluctant amusement. In a week or so, she might be happy to throw him into a room of his own.

CHAPTER NINE

'*No*, Jack!' Zac thundered as the toddler's fingers wandered too close to an electric socket.

Startled, Jack fell back on his bottom and burst into floods of tears. Zac scooped him up to comfort him while Freddie traced a piece of carving on the wooden panelling with awe-inspired admiration.

'That was dangerous,' Zac told Jack ruefully as the little boy gazed at him with hurt dark eyes and a trembling lower lip. 'And drop the pathetic look, you little chancer!'

'So, what do you think of this house?' Freddie asked with fake casualness.

Zac had been with Freddie long enough to recognise a trick question. Indeed, house-hunting with Freddie was an education. For such a practical woman, Freddie was very impractical when it came to houses. Only belatedly had he worked out that Freddie's dream house was ancient, in need of a great deal of tender loving care and somewhere buried in the country. He had the penthouse suite for convenience and business meetings in the City but it was anything but a comfortable base for raising two young children.

He had given Freddie brochures for houses that were immediately available for occupation but not a single 'wow' had escaped her lips until she had gone browsing on her own and discovered Mouldy Manor in Surrey. It was actually Molderstone Manor, he conceded grudgingly, but he preferred his own label for a property built on a shoestring in the Middle Ages and having since benefitted from a long line of penniless owners, who had been unable to afford restoration or modernisation.

'This house…it's different,' Zac selected tactfully. 'But it would be months before we could move into it.'

'But the north wing is liveable because it was rented out,' Freddie pointed out cheerfully. 'And we'd have plenty of bedroom space there. Jen and Izzy need their own space too.'

Their nannies had become Jen and Izzy, very much part of the family. Zac gritted his teeth at the reminder. He had forgotten about them. They needed more bedrooms than he had initially calculated and he didn't want to share their living space with staff round the clock. He watched Freddie caress the carved newel post of the staircase and almost groaned. 'We'll take another look at the north wing and see if it could be made habitable.'

'You realise that eventually you'll be living here alone?' Zac remarked, trudging round the two-storey north wing a second time, seeing every flaw in the tired décor and the paucity of bathrooms while Freddie waxed poetical about how quickly new bathrooms could be installed and how truly wonderful it was that the splendid plasterwork in the ceilings and walls had been preserved.

A sharp little silence fell and Freddie paled at that careless comment, that unwelcome reminder of the future that lay ahead in which Zac would walk away from her and the children. When he came back it would only be to maintain contact with the children. She wouldn't be his wife any more. She would only be the ex-wife in charge of the children and everything would be so very different. The reflection sobered her.

Only when he entered the extensive rear courtyard did Zac appreciate that Mouldy Manor could have unexpected possibilities. The stable block was enormous and the outbuildings were very good condition. 'I could ship over horses from the ranch and set up a breeding operation here,' he said then with surprising enthusiasm. 'We sell most of our most prized stallions to the Middle East.'

It was a gloriously sunny day and, determined not to spoil the day with anxious thoughts, Freddie unveiled the picnic she had brought in the overgrown garden, spreading a rug below a gnarled oak tree.

At that point, Zac recognised that a brutal opinion of Mouldy Manor would be deeply unwelcome. The children were running wild in the garden with Izzy following patiently in their wake, and Freddie was beaming as she cast long languishing looks back in the direction of the house every chance she got.

'It just says family to me,' she told him with enthusiasm. 'Even though it's big, it's got cosy spaces and I could do so much with those rooms. And look at Eloise and Jack enjoying the freedom to run wild outdoors...'

Zac duly looked, to discover that unsurprisingly the kids were doing their best to resemble storybook-perfect kids passing through a flower-strewn meadow in aid of Freddie's arguments. 'And we won't be tripping over staff here,' she pointed out, having already accepted that Zac would not live without, at the very least, a housekeeper and a cook.

Raised with domestic staff, Zac could imagine no other way of living. He didn't want his wife preoccupied with the necessities of life when he or the children wanted her attention. But Freddie found live-in staff intrusive and was only slowly adapting to her new luxury lifestyle.

'You could breed horses here,' she reminded him, relieved that he had found something to be positive about on the property.

They had been married for exactly eight weeks, having flown back from France on three separate occasions to attend adoption assessment sessions with the children. After the initial ructions, those seven weeks at the Villa Antonella had been blissfully happy. Zac had settled down and he hadn't shown any disappointment when her period had arrived within days of their wedding, confirming that she hadn't yet conceived.

That he wasn't impatient on that score was a plus, she reflected fondly. Yes, she *was* fond of him, she conceded, but fondness and love were two different things. She was fond of vanilla ice cream and even fonder of being wakened in the early hours by an insanely sexy masculine presence in her bed, but love she kept strictly focussed on the children. Zac was gorgeous and great company and many, many things she admired in a man.

He was amazingly patient with Eloise and Jack and, when Freddie had come down with a two-day virus, he had been kind in a way she had not expected him to be because those who rarely got ill usually weren't very sympathetic towards those who did. She had definitely made the right decision when she married him, she told herself happily. Of course, it would be a wrench when the time came for Zac to walk away, particularly if she didn't manage to give him a child and uphold her side of their bargain, but, knowing what lay ahead, she could prepare herself for that development. Practicality, not sentiment, she reminded herself resolutely, and there was no reason why she shouldn't enjoy their time together as a family, although sometimes she felt guilty at just how much she was enjoying being married to him.

'If you want this house, I'll buy it,' Zac breathed reluctantly.

'It's not your style, though.'

'I like the stables and I'm prepared to be persuaded,' Zac informed her, snaking out a strong arm as she knelt beside him and tipping her down onto his lap.

Freddie, demonstrating how much she had changed after two months of marriage, kissed him passionately and his arms tightened around her as he rocked her over the prominent bulge at his groin. A faint groan of frustration was wrenched from her as his arousal connected with the most intimate part of her.

'We could go back into the house and—'

'*Yes!*' she gasped with an eagerness she couldn't hide, and her cheeks reddened because just recently she couldn't seem to keep her hands off Zac and she was starting to wonder if that was quite normal or a sign that she was a little oversexed.

Zac laughed with rich appreciation. 'You really, *really* want this house.'

She gazed into his pale glittering black-lashed eyes, feeling her heart race at speed and her entire body heat to an embarrassing degree. 'I want you,' she contradicted without hesitation.

Being married wasn't so bad, Zac conceded, tugging his wife across the overgrown lawn to the house with one powerful hand. True, he had had to make explanations to Eloise about why he regularly forgot to wear pyjamas, and Jack, since he had learned how to climb out of his cot, allowed no such niceties to hold him back from a full-scale assault on the marital bed. Meal times had got messy but bath time was fun and bed time from an adult point of view was even more fun-filled, Zac acknowledged as he pinned Freddie to a wall and kissed her breathless, feeling as sexually voracious as a man who hadn't indulged in months, which would have been very untrue. But then Freddie acted on his libido like an aphrodisiac. Once was never enough and, now she was no longer as shy or nervous, she had become his dream lover, as enthusiastic and seemingly as sexually obsessed with him as he was with her. What was there not to like in that magical combination?

The skirt of her dress was up round her waist and there was a ripping sound as Zac impatiently dispensed with her skimpy silk knickers. She reckoned he preferred silk because it tore easily. Excitement sent her heart racing and her body pulsing as he unzipped, braced her back against the wall and suddenly he was there where she most needed him. She gasped and gasped again as he locked her legs round his waist to sink deeper into her slick, tender flesh. As he ground against her, possessing her with potent strength, carnal sensation pounded through her body in wave after wave until the pleasure rose to an unbearable crescendo and sent her flying high.

'You'll have to carry me back to the car,' she muttered after she had regained her voice, her head drooping down onto a broad shoulder for support. 'I'm done.'

'You can't be. You had an early night last night and you slept late this morning. I had to wake you for breakfast,' Zac reminded her, settling her down onto her own feet and bending down to retrieve her underwear and stuff it in his pocket.

Freddie swallowed back a yawn. 'You exhaust me...but in the nicest possible way,' she completed with a cheeky grin.

Zac made her pause before he opened the front door, long fingers combing through her tumbled hair to tidy it. But it made no perceptible difference. Her face was still pink from her climax and her eyes shone like stars. 'You still look like you've been thoroughly—'

'Pleasured is the word,' Freddie slotted in hastily, because Zac was trying to clean up his speech since Eloise had picked up a bad word after listening to him and if she had repeated that word once, she had repeated it a thousand times, making every adult in her radius cringe.

Zac looked down at Freddie and wished there were a bed within reach. 'Were you?'

'Thoroughly,' she told him, revelling in his spontaneous smile.

'By the way, there was something I've been meaning to discuss with you,' Zac told her in the back of the limo, Jen and Izzy and the children travelling in the car behind them. 'Who told you about the chalet girl in Klosters?'

Freddie grimaced. 'Her mother on our wedding day. I saw her with your father's party. He must have brought her, obviously not knowing how she felt about you.'

'I did first meet her in Dad's office with her mother and then she miraculously took a job at his ski retreat the week I was staying there with Vitale and Angel. She was a desperately pushy girl and I hate being hassled. I didn't sleep with her because if I had she would have clung like a limpet.'

'OK, so she lied to her mother and made you out to be the bad guy.'

'What did her mother say to you?' Zac demanded angrily.

'Pretty much that once you slept with a woman you lost interest.'

Zac's bright eyes gleamed with amusement. 'Well, you know that's not true where you're concerned.'

But it *would* be true in the future, Freddie thought unhappily, wondering why half the gloss had seemed to fall from her image of the house once she tried to imagine living there alone with the children. When it happened, it would be the end of their marriage and change was always scary, which was probably why her mind was so stubbornly refusing to stop thinking it. She wasn't even pregnant yet, she reminded herself, and who knew how long that would take? Or how long Zac would be willing to be patient? He never forgot what they shared was temporary but she forgot it over and over again.

Her face drenched with colour as she thought about the way they had made love in the house. Zac had few inhibitions but she had encouraged him. Should she really be demonstrating that much enthusiasm with a man who was planning to *leave* her? Shouldn't pride make her a little cooler? But how was she supposed to act cooler in that department when their main objective was for her to conceive? Torn apart by those conflicting thoughts, Freddie buried them. When their marriage was over, she told herself firmly, she would have to make her peace with reality.

The following day, Zac announced that Molderstone Manor was theirs with immediate possession and that he was throwing in a local construction firm to upgrade the north wing to his standards, which would allow the main house to be renovated at a more leisurely pace.

Freddie was thrilled and she hugged him and persuaded him that a second trip had to be made down to the manor. By the time surveys came back on the property, revealing that the manor was in much better order than Zac had anticipated, he was resigned to his future home and planning a helipad in the grounds for faster access. Freddie, however, immersed herself blissfully in paint colours and upholstery fabrics, leaving Zac to choose bathroom fittings and loudly veto some of her décor choices.

Another two weeks rattled past in that manner, by which time Zac was thoroughly bored with floral fabrics that sent Freddie into paroxysms of delight and convinced him that beige was the only way to go.

'Bland…bland…bland,' Freddie contradicted. 'It's not your fault. You're too used to living in hotels.'

She was sitting on the bed with a giant pile of fabric swatches. She had dug herself into the project of turning the big house into a home to lift her mood. As summer wore into autumn, the anniversary of her sister's tragic death loomed and she was keen to visit the cemetery where Lauren had been laid to rest, even though she knew it would reanimate sad memories. Tomorrow definitely, she decided ruefully, feeling guilty that she hadn't been back there since the funeral.

Zac swept the fabric swatches off the bed and pounced on her. 'You're not allowed to bring those to bed with you.'

'It's only eight o'clock in the evening. I'm not technically *in* bed,' Freddie pointed out, gazing up into black fringed stunning eyes that were the colour of grey ice in that light.

Zac wound his fingers slowly through the silky thickness of her hair. 'But I can put you there, *meu pequenino*,' he traded, in a dark deep drawl that sent tiny shivers of awareness down her spine. 'And keep you there.'

'Arrogant much?' Freddie mocked with dancing eyes.

And his mouth crushed hers in answer. He tasted of coffee and hunger and he smelt divine. It was one of those truly perfect moments that she cherished. The bedroom was an oasis of peace for her once the children were in bed but it was also a wildly exciting but safe place to be with Zac. Her arms closed round him as his tongue tangled with hers. She decided he deserved one beige room. She could live with beige in very small quantities.

The next morning, Freddie slept in yet again and got out of bed in a rush, wondering why on earth she should be so tired when she was doing so little. Throwing on clothes in haste and only a smidgeon of make-up, she brushed her hair and went to join Zac for breakfast. The minute she entered the big reception room the smell of fried food assailed her nostrils and her stomach performed a virtual somersault, which left her cramming her hand against her mouth and racing back to the bathroom, grateful that Zac was out on the balcony and shielded from the sight. There she was very sick and, sobered by the experience, she leant on the vanity counter studying her perspiring face with wide, troubled eyes. Now that she thought about it, and she really *hadn't* been thinking about it, she began counting days very carefully back to her last period. She was almost two weeks overdue! Could she be pregnant?

Of course you could be pregnant, you idiot, she scolded herself in exasperation. After all, they had been doing everything possible to get her pregnant since the day after they had married. A faint wave of warning dizziness engulfed her when she walked briskly back into the bedroom and she sat down with a still-swimming head on the end of the bed. Pregnant? *Pregnant!* She had thought it would take months to get pregnant, she had *assumed* it would take months but, possibly, not always. She headed back into the bathroom to clean her teeth and freshen up. She could be carrying Zac's baby right now.

How long would he stay with her once she told him? That single question sliced through every other thought in her head. Of course, she would have to check that she was pregnant first because she didn't want to sound a false alarm. And if she mentioned her suspicion to Zac, Zac would take over and she would be rushed off to see some fancy doctor when she could easily buy a pregnancy test and find out for herself. Would he stay with her at least until the baby was born? Freddie's lips quivered and her eyes prickled like mad. She didn't know what was wrong with her. Maybe it was her hormones. Would he even stay with her until the baby was a few months old? She sucked in a deep breath like a drowning swimmer, struggling to compose herself.

What Zac chose to do was not her business, she warned herself fiercely. They had an agreement. He had agreed to adopt Eloise and Jack with her and she had agreed to try and give him a child to enable him to take control of the da Rocha business empire. Obviously he couldn't leave her until the adoption was finalised, she acknowledged on a tide of sudden overpowering relief that even she couldn't ignore. And there was a couple of months yet to run on the adoption process.

Why did the prospect of Zac *leaving* fill her with horror and a deep and terrifying sense of abandonment? Practicality not sentiment, she rhymed to herself. Oh, to hell with that cop-out, she decided without hesitation. He was planning to desert her with two kids and another on the way and escape all the work and hassle of a newborn! How was *that* fair? Freddie hurtled at insane speed from misery to rage at the injustice of his plans.

This was the man she slept wrapped around every night. This was the man who enjoyed her body several times a day. This was the man planning to maroon her in the country with a house that needed a

heck of a lot of work and someone with Zac's drive
and energy to ensure it got done! That Molderstone
Manor happened to be her dream house should carry
no weight in the argument, she told herself, determined to be a martyr in every way.

'What's up?' Zac enquired lazily as Freddie tilted
her nose in the air and walked to the far end of the
balcony, turning her slender back to him.

'Nothing's up,' she responded, taking in a great
gulp of fresh air to close out the faint aroma of fried
food still on the table.

'Aren't you joining me for breakfast?'

'I'm not hungry. Where are the children?'

'Izzy took them to the park.' Zac appraised her
as she turned. She looked very pale and the tip of
her nose was pink as if she had been crying. 'Have
you been crying?'

'Why would I have been crying?' Freddie asked
stiffly. 'I've got some shopping to do.'

'I'm meeting Dad for lunch but I can do shopping as long as neither paint nor fabric choices are
involved.' Zac sprang upright, every long, lean line
of his powerful body defined by the beautifully tailored navy suit he wore teamed with a forest-green
shirt and a silk tie. 'You're like a headless chicken
when you shop. You can never make your mind up
about anything.'

'I'd rather go alone,' Freddie muttered, biting at
her lip. 'Because afterwards I'm planning to visit

the cemetery where my sister is buried. It's the anniversary of her death.'

'Why am I only hearing about that now?' Zac queried, relieved to have grasped what had probably caused the tears he suspected. 'You know, you hardly ever mention her.'

'Doesn't mean I don't miss her. She was so good to me when I was a kid. But everything went wrong for her,' Freddie responded tightly, suddenly dangerously on the edge of tears again.

'She'd be proud of what you're doing for her children.'

Freddie said nothing because sadly her last memories of her sister only reminded her that Lauren would have sacrificed anything and anybody for her next fix. Lauren had been too lost in drugs to care about her children.

'I'm definitely coming with you to the cemetery,' Zac decreed. 'Give me a time and we'll meet up.'

Freddie gave way on that point and headed straight out to buy a pregnancy test at the pharmacy only down the road. She then retreated back to the hotel cloakroom to get the test done. Well, actually, the *three* tests done because she didn't want to get all worked up about a possible mistake, did she? And, one after another, each test put up an unmistakeable positive and tears rolled down her cheeks. And she hated herself but she hated Zac even more for getting her pregnant so quickly. She should be happy that she had conceived and somehow that aspect had been stolen from her by their situation.

Why was that? she asked herself. Shouldn't she be rushing back up to the penthouse in the lift and sharing her good news? Zac would want to celebrate. He would be surprised it had happened so quickly for them. As he had said weeks back when she had realised that she hadn't conceived. 'We're not in a hurry.' Of course, he had had to say that, hadn't he? He didn't want her to feel stressed out about the conception plan, having already mentioned that stress wouldn't aid that goal. How had *he* known that? Had he been reading up about pregnant women?

She looked down at her flat tummy and tried to imagine a little jumping bean like Jack nestling inside her and warm acceptance spread through her at last. A little Zac or a little girl, she didn't care, only that it would be *his* child. And that was the point when it finally dawned on her that she was head over heels in love with her husband. She had broken the rules! She had gone and fallen for him in spite of all his warnings and against all common sense. The tears bubbled up again and she blinked them angrily away.

She was happy about the baby but terrified of losing Zac, and her pregnancy had to mean the beginning of the end for their marriage. There, now she knew what was wrong with her. It was fear of the massive changes ahead of her, of rebuilding a life that would seem empty without him. No more Zac. No more smiles or jokes or kisses. No more unexpected gifts. No more envious looks from other women. No more stories about Brazil. She would never visit Brazil now. Zac had been planning to take her there once the adoption was finalised but it wouldn't happen now. She had missed that boat.

She would never see the horse ranch where he had spent his early years. She would never meet his grandmother on the Amazonian rubber plantation where the old lady still lived in her retirement. She would never attend the carnival in Rio with him or see the beautiful women strolling along Copacabana beach in scanty swimwear, whom Zac had admitted fantasising about as a teenager. He had shared so much with her about his background and homeland but now he would never take her to Brazil because she was pregnant and what would be the point? From now on he would see everything through the prism of the reality that he would soon be splitting up with her.

Dear heaven, would he expect her to be all jolly and friendly about the divorce? Well, she would look like an idiot if she got upset and he realised she had become extremely attached to him. She remembered the young woman in Klosters whom he had shunned for fear that, given encouragement, she would cling to him like a limpet. Freddie had no desire to be Zac's limpet in life. She would be strong and sensible. She wouldn't let him guess how she felt.

Zac was waiting at the cemetery gates for her with his bodyguards. He told her off for not using the limo or taking her bodyguard out with her.

'I felt like a walk alone,' she mumbled, walking through the gates with only the hum of a mower and the traffic beyond the walls infiltrating the emptiness.

'It was such a waste. She was so young,' she told him as she laid down her flowers and backed away to sit on a bench nearby.

Zac didn't voice any of the empty clichés that were often utilised in such moments. He settled down beside her and closed a soothing arm round her taut shoulders.

'I still feel so guilty,' Freddie admitted convulsively. 'I kind of used to blame her for falling into drugs but, the last year of her life, she told me something that has haunted me ever since. I wish she had told me a lot sooner and then I would've understood better, but she thought I was too young and she didn't want to upset me.'

'What did she tell you?' Zac prompted when the silence dragged on.

'We were put in a care home the first few weeks after our parents died.' Freddie struggled to control her turbulent emotions. 'When Lauren was pregnant with Jack, she told me that she was raped there but she didn't report it because she was threatened and she was scared something would happen to me. It's so ugly.'

'But not your fault. You were a child,' Zac soothed.

'You see, she changed but I didn't know why. Wherever we were she looked after me like a mother hen and then, when she got old enough to leave foster care, she fell in with a bad set of people and everything went downhill after that. She couldn't cope with life on her own.'

'You did everything you could to help her,' Zac interposed. 'Freddie… I've lost friends to drugs and not everyone is capable of what it takes to get clean. I think you need to believe that she's gone to a better place and forgive yourself for not being able to save her.'

'Yes,' she mumbled tearfully, loving him so much at that instant that she almost sobbed all over him.

'And perhaps we could get her a nicer headstone,' Zac suggested lightly.

'It was the best we could afford at the time. Claire paid for everything. Gosh, I still owe her the money for that.' Freddie sighed.

'I'll take care of it. Shall I wait at the gates for you?' Zac asked. 'Maybe you'd like to spend a few minutes here on your own.'

Nodding jerkily, Freddie watched the love of her life stride away, tall and straight and full of innate power and confidence. Lauren had said that Cruz was 'the one' for her and Freddie, who had never been in love, hadn't really understood the strength of such emotions, had not grasped that her sister simply didn't have the power to break away from her toxic boyfriend. But she understood now.

And for the first time she saw a clear path in front of her. One of the elements she most valued in her relationship with Zac was the level of honesty with which they dealt with each other. She had to tell him that she was pregnant immediately, she decided heavily. She couldn't keep secrets from him. But she *could* act on her own behalf like a strong, independent woman and walk away first.

It would hurt like hell, she knew it would, but at least it would cut out any 'will he, won't he?' scenarios in which she hoped for more from him than he wanted to give. If she made the first move, there would be no humiliating emotional scenes between them and their relationship would remain stable in the future, which was very important from the children's point of view.

Zac, after all, hadn't shifted an inch in his attitude towards their marriage. It wasn't even fair for her to expect more from him. He was good to her, *really* good, but he didn't love her, nor did he want to keep her for ever. Sadly, she wasn't 'the one' for Zac da Rocha, because if she had been he would surely have said something after two months of marriage. Instead he was still reminding her that what they had was a temporary marriage.

Her mind made up, Freddie rose from the bench to leave the cemetery.

CHAPTER TEN

'I HAVE NEWS for you,' Freddie announced with false bravado when she climbed into the limousine with Zac. 'I'm pregnant.'

'How do you know? I mean…' perplexed, Zac stared at her, black brows drawn together '…are you certain?'

'Well, I haven't seen a doctor yet, but I've done *three* pregnancy tests,' she told him.

Zac continued to stare at her, evidently astonished by her announcement. 'We'll make an appointment for today.'

'Maybe for tomorrow. That would be time enough. I'm only about six or seven weeks along at most,' she pointed out. 'So, there you are, we've done it!'

'I wasn't prepared for it to happen so soon,' Zac admitted tautly. 'But it's wonderful news.'

'Yes,' Freddie agreed. 'Hopefully by the middle of next year, you'll be sitting in the CEO chair of the da Rocha business empire. Bearing that in mind, I think it's time that we take stock of our situation and make plans for the future.'

Their *situation*? Zac didn't like that description of their marriage. He studied Freddie's flat stomach, striving to imagine a baby in there. *His* baby! He was transfixed by the concept until he recalled the many pregnancy complications that had assailed his mother. Every time he'd seen her, she had either been pregnant or just getting over another heartbreaking loss. Something very like panic attacked Zac as he looked at Freddie's fragile little body and thought in horror of all that could go wrong. *Run*, don't walk, to the doctor, he decided instantly.

'I would very much prefer you to see a doctor today, *meu pequenino*,' Zac told her squarely, wanting her tested and screened and scanned within an inch of her life at every stage of her pregnancy.

'Once we've decided what comes next,' Freddie agreed for the sake of peace as they walked back into The Palm Tree. 'Could we go into the bar for a while? I'd love a cappuccino.'

Zac glanced at her in surprise because she normally avoided the bar where she had once worked. But Freddie wanted a public space free of children in which to talk to Zac and the bar was the most convenient option. It was even better that he would soon have to leave to meet his father for lunch.

Within minutes they were seated out on the quiet terrace, free of the lunchtime crowds.

Zac was already on his phone, talking to Angel about which obstetrician Merry was seeing while she was in London. Obtaining the number, he rang and made an appointment for late afternoon. Only then did he give Freddie his full attention.

'I think we need a little distance from each other now,' Freddie informed him with a resolutely cheerful smile. 'I want to move straight into Molderstone and supervise the work there. I know the adoption application is still ongoing but you can visit whenever you like and you've got to admit that the penthouse is hopeless for the kids.'

Zac felt as if someone had crept up behind him with a large plank and bashed him on the head without warning. Her proposal had zero appeal for him. 'But—'

'It's what I want. My own space with the kids. I've hopefully met the terms of our agreement and our marriage is on the way out now.'

'It didn't feel like it was on the way out last night,' Zac was goaded into protesting.

Her colour rising at the reminder, Freddie gave him a steely appraisal. 'But we have to put that kind of stuff in the past now and work on establishing a friendly, platonic relationship.'

Zac tried hard to credit that this version of Freddie was still *his* Freddie. Native caution kept him silent. The minute she conceived, she wanted to ditch him, deprive him of the kids and move miles away to her dream house, which was probably anything but a dream house, full of workmen as it currently was. What had come over her? But she *said* this was what she wanted. Zac was in shock.

'You were keen for us to maintain a good relationship after we parted,' Freddie reminded him ruefully.

That was true, Zac conceded as he struggled to breathe evenly with a constricted chest.

'You want your freedom back,' Freddie continued.

That was true, *wasn't it*? Zac's mind was a blank at that definitive moment. All he could see in his brain was Freddie versus freedom in block capital letters although he wouldn't be moving with them.

'And just think of how free you'll be with all of us out of your hair!' Freddie invited with yet another bright smile, as if she could hardly wait to get on the road and away from him.

A ghastly suspicion occurred to Zac then. Maybe right from the start Freddie had craved exactly this conclusion; maybe she wasn't as uninterested in his wealth as she had pretended. She had money now, a new home, and Eloise and Jack were well on the way to becoming theirs. She had kept her part of the bargain and now it was time for him to hold up his end of the deal. He didn't like the idea of *his* baby being part of a deal, but when she was so eager as to call time on their marriage the very same day that she found out she was pregnant, it was clear that she wanted *her* freedom back and had no hesitation in demanding it.

He was so angry with her that he didn't trust himself to speak. He could barely credit that only the night before they had been arguing about colour schemes for the house she was now planning to occupy without him. Or maybe her motivation was even more basic, he reasoned. Maybe she didn't like him or being married to him, which made her a heck of a good actress and him a sentimental idiot, he conceded grimly.

'Zac…?' Freddie prompted.

'We'll see Merry's obstetrician this afternoon and you can leave first thing in the morning,' Zac drawled stonily, his jaw line clenched, the exotic slant of his cheekbones flushed below eyes as cold as Siberian ice.

Freddie hesitated and weakness shot straight into the gap in her concentration.

'This is what you want as well, *isn't it*?' she pressed.

'It's pretty much what we agreed,' Zac conceded carelessly, and then he drained his expresso in one unappreciative gulp and sprang back upright, all leashed vitality and masculine restlessness. 'Look, I'd better make a move if I don't want to keep my father waiting. He hates it if you're late.'

'Give him my love.'

Zac froze and turned a chilling look on her. 'Bit pointless now, isn't it? You're on the way out of the family.'

Freddie sucked in a great shuddering breath as he

strode off the terrace. She had believed he would be happier about both the pregnancy and her plans to move back out of his life. Instead he seemed angry, hostile, almost bitter. Was that because she had taken him by surprise when she had taken the lead for a change in making a major decision? She supposed it must be. Zac liked to do things at his own pace in his own way and he had been disconcerted and annoyed by her sudden decision. She wanted to weep into her cappuccino like a limp weed of a woman but she didn't. Instead, she went back upstairs to lunch with the children and pretend that she had not a care in the world.

Late afternoon, Zac reappeared to take her to the obstetrician's appointment. A lot of tests were carried out before she was ushered into Mr Simonides's presence. He confirmed her pregnancy and gave her a scan. Freddie stared rigidly at the screen, both she and Zac behaving rather like two strangers forced to share a waiting room. She wasn't used to Zac being quiet or cold and it unnerved her. The steady beat of their baby's heart broke the silence and her eyes welled up with helpless tears of awe as she concentrated on the screen showing nothing as yet recognisable as a baby.

'That's it?' Zac stood up to move closer and asked several questions, demonstrating more interest and knowledge than she had expected.

When she walked back out onto the street, Zac

wiped his damp eyes and said gruffly, 'That was fascinating. I won't miss a single appointment,' he swore.

And then, his cold façade having cracked for that split second, he got down on his knees with Eloise and Jack and patiently explained that they were moving to the house in the country where they had had the picnic but that, although he wouldn't be moving with them, they would still see lots of him. Jack didn't understand a word of that explanation but Eloise burst into tears, and Zac shot Freddie an accusing glance and hugged the little girl. A few minutes later, Zac stood up, announced that he was going out and didn't know how late he would be back but that he might not see them before they left in the morning.

Freddie was shocked by that news. It was as if Zac was rushing out of the door to reclaim his precious freedom while she was stuck for the evening with a grieving Eloise and a nauseous tummy that nothing would settle. She didn't sleep a wink that night.

The north wing was in a huge mess with builders' supplies stacked everywhere, but the required number of bedrooms and bathrooms and a temporary kitchen space were functional and Freddie gritted her teeth and got on with settling in. It was very unfortunate that she had never learned to drive because Jen had to take her shopping in the nearest town. Driving lessons were a must, she registered, and she was lucky she had the children to keep her focussed. Unfortunately, however, the name 'Zac' was flung at her by Eloise and even Jack multiple times a day, and just forty-eight hours after leaving London Freddie was struggling to cope and stay strong.

Leaving Zac had cut her in two. She had not appreciated how much she depended on him until he was gone from her life. All the sunshine in her world had evaporated. There was nothing to look forward to but the baby and the baby was making her very, very sick. The children were miserable and so was she. She fought to keep busy and tried to stop dwelling on the loss of him. After all, he would have left her anyway, and at least this way she had chosen the timing.

Zac lounged back in his usual seat on the bar terrace and drank his coffee because he was definitely feeling a little the worse for wear. Two late nights on the town in succession had drained him and coming home to the empty penthouse hadn't helped.

Freddie occupied every one of his thoughts and it was driving him insane. He remembered his first glimpse of her in the bar, the instant lust she had inspired in him. He pictured her delivering drinks, the fluid glide of her walk that by late evening would be stiff because her feet were hurting her, the cheeky grin that lit up her face when someone made her laugh, the warmth in her eyes when she looked

at him. No, that was a much later memory, he reminded himself. There had been no warmth those
first weeks, only distrust and wariness, and that was
hardly surprising when he considered the crude way
he had first approached her.

Regret and frustration coursed through Zac in
violent waves. A woman had never walked out on
him before. Could it really have been that his money
was his sole attraction in her eyes? But the minute he considered that idea, he dismissed it again.
Freddie was the woman who had offered to set him
free the day after their wedding, even though that
could well have meant that she lost the children and
it would have seriously reduced any financial support she was entitled to receive from him. Freddie
didn't have a greedy bone in her body. She had put
his needs before her own that day, he finally acknowledged with regret.

What if she was doing that again? Giving *him*
what she thought *he* wanted and needed?

That idea shot a bright clarifying light through
Zac's dark brooding thoughts and a moment later
he was on his feet and heading back up to the penthouse. It was a dull, overly silent and depressing
space without Freddie and the children. He hated it.
He hated waking up alone in bed as well. He hated
lying about why she and the children had left London. To say that Freddie was supervising the builders was a joke because Freddie knew as much about

building as he did about cooking, but for the sake of the adoption they had to keep up the illusion that they were a perfectly happy married couple...which meant that when he turned up, she wouldn't *dare* turn him away from the door!

Energised by that certainty, Zac went for a shower, decided not to waste time shaving and packed a bag, including several gifts he had bought earlier that day. He didn't want to be that kind of father though, one who visited rarely and brought presents to grease his passage. He enjoyed the daily hurly-burly of young children, recognising only now how very unnatural his own lonely upbringing had been on the ranch. He had spent half his life fiercely resenting the inheritance trust that would force him to have a child, only to discover late in the day that he liked children and that the sight of that tiny life on the screen at the doctor's had filled him with longing.

And now that he had a pregnant wife, he *should* be with her to look after her. What craziness had persuaded Freddie that she could dispense with him at such an important and dangerous time? But then Freddie wasn't very practical, Zac conceded, although she liked to think she was and he wasn't going to be the one to disabuse her of that false conviction. Freddie was a romantic, an idealist, and she had a heart as big as the planet, always looking out for others ahead of herself. He hoped she had some space left in that heart for the deeply flawed husband she had deserted. There was nothing he wouldn't do or say or utilise to get her back. Zac smiled for the first time in three days. He had always done well with a steep challenge...

As Zac climbed into a helicopter to travel to Molderstone Manor, Freddie was freaking out because the water had gone off just as she'd stepped into the shower and she badly needed to wash her hair. She'd clambered out again to find that Jack had emptied the bathroom cupboard and spilled everything everywhere while Eloise happily sprayed herself with Freddie's expensive perfume. Jen was in bed with the flu and it was Izzy's day off. Zac would have asked Izzy to pick another day but Freddie, knowing that the nanny hadn't seen her boyfriend for two weeks, couldn't bring herself to inflict that disappointment on the young woman.

Getting dressed again in her jeans and a clean tee shirt, Freddie wound a scarf through her hair to tie it out of her way and marvelled at how fast her sartorial standards had fallen. There was no Zac to dress for any more, no need for silk lingerie that only reminded her of things she would sooner forget. Gathering up the children, she went to check on Jen and found her asleep, which would probably do more to speed her recovery than anything else.

She had set up the big room off the kitchen, which was intended as a reception room, as a playroom for the kids, a safe space where neither could come to harm. She busied herself making chicken nuggets and chips for the kids and felt very guilty about it, but she needed Jen hale and hearty to drive her to the supermarket and she had to manage with what was in the freezer. If only she could manage herself half as well, she thought wretchedly, because she was so tired she could have lain down and slept on the tiles under her bare feet.

At least the fried food wasn't upsetting her to the same extent any longer and the nausea did tend to come in the morning and the ginger tea did seem to help a little. She winced as someone began hammering at a wall again and then the sound of a saw started up and she gritted her teeth. It was *her* choice to be here while the work went on, although in truth she couldn't follow the plans the master builder liked to spread in front of her every morning without fail while he shared his plans and acknowledged the problems he was having.

When Zac walked into the kitchen, she was munching on a half-cooked oven chip, and in shock at his sudden appearance she almost swallowed it whole. He looked so achingly familiar in black jeans and a dark green shirt that accentuated every lean line of his muscular physique. And *she* looked such a mess. Stupid to care about that, a little voice sniped inside her, but she did care at being caught without make-up with her hair in her mess and wearing her oldest clothes.

'I thought it was time I came for a visit,' he told her, his gaze roaming over her very slowly as though he didn't quite recognise her, and probably he didn't because she looked dreadful.

'You should've phoned, given me some warning. I hope you've eaten already because we're out of food,' she told him shakily, battling to steady herself and rise to the challenge of greeting Zac as if he were merely an old friend.

'How can you be out of food?' he demanded, and she explained about her not being able to drive and Jen being ill and Izzy off while his lean, darkly handsome face grew more and more grim.

About then she noticed the silence and peered out of the door. 'Where are the builders?'

'I told them to pack up for the day.'

'Oh…' Freddie could think of nothing to say to that, beyond, 'Maybe the water's back on!'

And mercifully it was, she discovered by dint of turning on a tap. By then Zac's presence had drawn Eloise and Jack and they threw themselves at him as if he had been absent for weeks rather than days. He produced a bag from the hall behind him and dug into it to bestow a fluffy unicorn on Eloise, her latest craze, and some kind of robot ball that was self-propelled, and which Jack immediately went off to chase round the room.

'I want to forget about the agreement we made before we married,' Zac informed her.

'But why?' she asked uncertainly.

'Because I've changed and I'm hoping you've changed too.' Zac rested his stunning eyes on her, thinking that she looked frazzled and feeling guilty because he had allowed that to happen when he was responsible for her well-being.

'What way have you changed?' she asked nervously.

'You changed my priorities. I don't want my freedom back. I've had ten years of complete freedom and it didn't bring me half as much happiness as you and the children have in two months. Two months of you wasn't enough,' he added, in case she had still not caught his drift because she was staring back at him with an expression as blank as a clean page.

'So…er…' Thoroughly confused by that speech, because her tired brain was malfunctioning, Freddie fumbled for words. 'You don't want a divorce any more?' she checked.

Zac lunged at the oven as the smell of burning assailed him, and grabbed up a dishcloth to pull a smoking selection of burning nuggets out of the oven.

'Auntie forgot them again,' Eloise told him forlornly. 'I'm hungry but now they burnt.'

'No problem.' Zac dug out his phone and spoke to his bodyguards. 'We'll order in tonight. What would you like, *meu pequenino*?'

'Anything,' she framed, too tied up in noticing that he hadn't answered her question about the divorce he had originally planned. 'But there isn't much choice of takeout round here.'

'Marco will find us something. We won't go hungry,' Zac declared, gathering Eloise up in his arms. 'Now, why don't you go and get some rest while I look after these two?'

'I can't do that.'

'Yes, you can. You're ready to pass out standing up and you shouldn't be in that condition,' Zac told her censoriously. 'You're supposed to be looking after yourself but, by the looks of it, you're not doing it very well.'

'Always the soul of tact!' Freddie snapped back at him, her colour roused, her brown eyes angry. 'I have bad days and good days and this has been one of the bad ones.'

'Which is why you need to lie down and let me take care of things,' Zac interjected impatiently.

The nagging tiredness that Freddie realised was a feature of early pregnancy, and which reduced her brain to mush, pushed Freddie up the stairs to the bedroom. He would ensure the kids ate and for one night it really didn't matter if they went to bed in the wrong pyjamas or he let them eat unhealthy stuff. But, exhausted as she was, she still trudged into the bathroom. She turned on the shower to check that both water supply and heating element were functioning before she washed herself from head to toe, slowly mulling over what Zac had said. Did the three of them make Zac happy? Had he missed them? Or had he simply missed the constant supply of sex? Was it possible that he had changed?

She fell into bed with hair that was still damp and thought about how she had changed. She had been so sure that she could keep control of her emotions and yet she had failed dismally. *She* had changed, learning what it was like to love someone even if she hadn't realise that she had loved him at the time and then learning what it was like to lose him again. She must've loved Zac when she'd offered him that annulment because she hadn't been able to bear the idea of him feeling trapped and unhappy in their marriage. Unable to reach a conclusion, she let sleep take over.

When she wakened again, it was dark outside and the bedside lamp was lit. Zac rose from the chair in the corner. 'Are you hungry?'

'Yes, but—'

'I'll bring you something.' And he was gone and clattering down the stairs before she could say another word.

She checked her watch. She had been asleep for hours. It was after eleven now and Zac was still on the premises, which meant that he was definitely staying the night. Her hopes rose exponentially and by the time he came back upstairs with a tray she was able to smile more normally at him. She looked down at the perfectly presented steak and salad in surprise.

'Marco. He used to be a chef,' Zac explained. 'He couldn't find a decent takeout place, so he bought food and cooked it for all of us, including Jen.'

Freddie picked up her knife and fork. 'Do you or do you not still want a divorce?' she demanded bluntly.

Zac leant back against the wall by the door. '*Don't*…don't want to lose you,' he extended with precision.

'And when did this change take place?' Freddie asked helplessly, because she was afraid to believe in what he was saying. 'Only a few days ago, you were telling me that—'

'I didn't know I'd changed until you walked out. I wasn't exactly on the ball with that,' Zac conceded with a sardonic twist of his mouth that could have signified embarrassment. 'I was just sailing along from day to day with you, perfectly happy, and then you exploded me out of my comfort zone.'

'By telling you that I was pregnant?' Freddie prodded.

'No, by *leaving me*,' Zac emphasised. 'I want you back. I have this big Freddie-shaped hole in my life and nothing other than you will fill it. I'm sorry that it took me so long to realise how I felt about you, but I was enjoying myself far too much with you to waste my energy psychoanalysing my…er…emotions.'

Freddie tried hard not to smile. 'And how long did it take you to work out that little speech?'

'The whole trip here,' Zac admitted with a grimace.

Freddie bent down to set the tray on the floor, her appetite having receded. She rested back against the pillows and surveyed him. He was nervous, long brown fingers clenching and unclenching, his glorious eyes intent on her. 'And how do you feel about me?'

'I love you. I've never said that to a woman before. I've never felt what you make me feel and I want to hang onto it with both hands,' he confessed in a driven undertone. 'I have a question for you.'

'No, if you tell me you love me, you have to throw yourself on the bed and kiss me passionately,' Freddie instructed gently. 'Then you can ask all the questions you like.'

An unholy grin lit up Zac's unusually sombre features and he stalked as fluidly as a jungle cat across the room to throw himself down on the bed with alacrity. 'This is why I love you. You always say the right thing at the right time…like asking me to do what I want to do anyway.'

Freddie leant primly forward, keeping the duvet locked beneath her arms, as if making it clear that a kiss was all she was offering. His big hands spread across her cheekbones, his beautiful eyes full of tenderness. 'You don't believe me yet, do you?' he guessed.

'I'm working on it,' she mumbled, and then he kissed her and she fell into that kiss like ice cream sliding down a hot griddle, both hands clutching the front of his shirt as if she would never let him go again. She tasted him and savoured him, her head falling back as he ravaged her mouth with all the hunger she welcomed.

'So that question…' Zac dragged out the last word, his attention welded to the lush, inviting line of her swollen mouth. 'Did you walk out because you assumed that that would make me happy? Or were you teaching me a lesson?'

'I thought it would make you happy and cut out the emotional awkwardness of you having to tell me you wanted a divorce at some point. I really wasn't trying to teach you a lesson.'

'Even though I deserved it after all the times I told you *not* to fall in love with me? Please tell me you didn't listen. Please tell me that you feel the same way and that I can keep you for good,' he breathed raggedly.

'Yes, I love you, of course, I do,' she soothed him, running a gentle fingertip along the tense and vulnerable line of his full lower lip. 'I really, *really* love you and I want to be with you for ever.'

'For ever and ever and ever, like in a fairy story. You're too good for me. I've never been good. I'm often selfish. I suffer from tunnel vision. I married you sincerely believing in everything I said about our agreement and then you made me want so much more. In fact you *gave* me so much more I couldn't get enough of it or you,' he confessed in a shaken undertone. 'Your warmth, your open heart, your kindness, your sense of fun.'

'Getting a hugely swollen head here!' she warned, tears of happiness running down her cheeks.

'Why are you crying?' Zac demanded.

'Because I'm happy and I was *so* unhappy without you!' she confided convulsively on the back of a sob. 'I truly believed we were over.'

'Never. I missed you and Eloise and Jack far too much to stay away. I was lonely. I've been lonely all my life but I'm not lonely when I have you three as my family. The children are in bed, by the way,' he added. 'But Eloise insisted on wearing her princess dress to bed and Jack screamed the place down when I tried to separate him from that stupid toy I brought him, so I switched it off so it won't fire up and wake him in the middle of the night,' Zac told her. 'It plays the most horrible tunes over *and* over again.'

'He'll be bored with it by tomorrow,' Freddie forecast. 'Do you really want the children as well as me? I mean, I could never turn my back on them but you didn't sign up for that.'

'I fell in love with them too and it's largely getting

to know Eloise and Jack that has encouraged me to feel that I can hardly wait to meet our baby,' Zac admitted reflectively, spreading his fingers across her flat stomach, the heat of his skin burning through the loose tee she wore to bed. 'They've taught me the basics. I'll be more useful by the time the third arrives.'

He had let the last of his barriers down and now he trusted and valued them enough to love them. She wanted to tell him that he had a warm, loving heart too, but sensed he wouldn't accept it yet though she saw that generous acceptance in his attitude to Eloise and Jack.

'I have one more confession to make,' Zac declared abruptly, resting back from her and withdrawing his caressing hand. 'And I should've made it months ago when you confronted me about it.'

'The two women at the royal ball?' Freddie exclaimed, frowning. 'I don't want to talk about that *ever*. It was your lowest moment.'

Zac winced. 'Even if nothing happened?'

'Nothing?' Freddie looked at him in open disbelief.

'I saved face at the expense of your feelings,' Zac admitted guiltily. 'Nothing happened because I didn't want either of them. I only wanted *you* and I only get turned on by you. I was too proud to tell you that at the time but I hurt you and I'm sorry for it.'

Freddie flung herself on top of him, finally convinced that he loved her because he had broken through his macho conditioning to tell her the truth. She wrapped both arms round his neck and Zac took it from there. He made love to her with all the passionate tenderness and smouldering sexiness she had learned to crave from him, but it was so much sweeter an experience when he was telling her that he loved her and holding her close in the aftermath, without feeling the need to pretend that she was the one forcing affection on him.

The toy ball woke Jack up in the middle of the night and his screams wakened the whole household, and the following day it was clear that Jack was scared of the ball because he wouldn't go near it and it had to be put away. Eloise arrived at dawn with her unicorn and her new unicorn story book and settled herself carefully between her future parents for over an hour. She was still wearing her princess dress and only gave it up when Freddie threatened to put her in the bath in it.

EPILOGUE

ON THE LAWN of Molderstone Manor, Jack, who was two and a half now, was playing ball. He was turning into an athletic little boy, Freddie mused, smiling as Eloise sat down to play with her little sister, Antonella, who was trying to crawl on her rug and not getting very far. It was a glorious sunny day and it was her youngest daughter Antonella's first birthday.

As she basked in the heat the past eighteen months played through Freddie's memory in fast and colourful images, crowded with milestones of happiness. To celebrate the adoption of Eloise and Jack, they had travelled to Brazil and had enjoyed a fabulous holiday, while also visiting Zac's elderly grandmother, Maria. Antonella had been born before that summer really took off and she was an adaptable baby with a nature as sunny and smiley as Jack's. Her hair was dark, her skin the colour of milk coffee and she looked very much like her namesake.

Zac had fussed a lot over Freddie during her pregnancy and she had been relieved that she had suffered none of the crises or complications that his late mother had endured. In fact her pregnancy had been relatively easy and the delivery straightforward. She suspected that if they decided to have another child, Zac would be considerably less prone to panic the second time around. Regardless, she was happier than she had ever hoped she could be, the shadows of past loss and pain finally laid to rest by both of them.

After their daughter's birth Zac had become CEO of the vast da Rocha business empire and during the months that followed he had flown from one end of the globe to the other, settling into his new role. Eventually he had taken Angel's advice and had hired several executive managers so that he could spend more time at home, or at least base most of his work in London. Molderstone Manor had blossomed since their first viewing and they were all now comfortably accommodated in the main house, where Zac enjoyed every comfort he craved amidst the floral fabrics he had learned to live with. His office, however, was strictly beige and functional.

The breeding stables he had established with the support of the Brazilian staff he had brought in were already doing very well. Freddie had taken a Montessori diploma course during the months that Zac was travelling most, knowing it would be useful to her when she was raising three children. Her aunt,

Claire, had married her boyfriend earlier that year and Zac and Freddie had flown out to the wedding in Spain.

Jazz, now the Queen of Lerovia, strolled out of the house with her twins, Abramo and Chiara, tucked into a double buggy and walked over to join Freddie with the lack of ceremony that Freddie liked most about Zac's family. They all visited each other's homes, they all relaxed in those homes as if they were their own and, in making that effort to stay in regular contact, their husbands were getting closer and their children were growing up together.

'Where's Merry?' Freddie enquired sleepily.

'She decided to take a nap while Cosmas is down for his,' Jazz told her, for Merry's second child was a newborn and had not yet settled into a regular sleep pattern. 'And Vitale and Angel are hanging around the barbecue with Charles acting like grilling a hamburger is rocket science. Sybil's with them too.'

Merry's grandmother was Charles's girlfriend and rarely strayed from his side.

'It's so wonderfully peaceful here.' Jazz sighed, sinking down into a seat in the shade.

'Famous last words!' Freddie laughed as the racket of a helicopter disturbed the peace.

'Zac?'

'I hope so.' Freddie peered up at the sky but couldn't read the logo and then the craft circled and lowered, making identification unnecessary.

'Go and meet him,' Jazz urged. 'I'll watch Antonella.'

Freddie pelted at speed across the grass towards the helipad. Zac had been touring the mines in South Africa and Russia for two weeks and each week had felt like a month. Late-night phone calls hadn't made up for his absence. Zac sprang out of the helicopter and she raced into his arms.

'Missed you so much!' She gasped as he grabbed her up into his arms, the familiar scent and feel of him washing over her like a healing drug.

'And I missed you too,' Zac groaned, staring down at her smiling face with a wealth of love and appreciation.

He tasted her ripe pink mouth with sexy, hungry brevity and gazed down at her with devouring crystalline eyes.

'No, we can't,' she told him as if he had asked a question, scanning his lean, darkly handsome features with a heady combination of longing and admiration. 'Later.'

'Why do we have two nannies?' Zac breathed in exasperation.

'We have your family here. Right now, we're hosts and we are not sneaking off like randy teenagers,' she declared. 'Lift a beer and be sociable round the barbecue instead.'

'I want you so much,' Zac husked in Portuguese and she could feel her bones turning to water, but at the same time she was also remembering the cracks the last time they had disappeared at such an event and the ensuing embarrassment. Sadly, Zac didn't get embarrassed about stuff of that nature. 'And I promise to make you very, *very* happy.'

'You always do,' she muttered as they returned to Jazz and the three babies.

'I was expecting you two to disappear,' Jazz told them cheerfully. 'You're famous for that.'

'Well, we've grown up a bit,' Freddie told her sister-in-law piously.

'You may have,' Zac said levelly. 'But I *haven't*.'

And with that statement, Zac swung Freddie up into his arms and carried her indoors, impervious to Angel taunting him from the barbecue. Ignoring her protests, he carried her upstairs to their bedroom and fell down on the bed with her, lamenting that she would need to go on a diet before he would try that again. Freddie thumped him with a pillow and then, suddenly, he was flattening her to the mattress and gazing down at her with an urgency that sent heat coursing through her lower limbs.

'I love you so much, *meu pequenino*,' he told her with raw sincerity. 'It's hell being away from you for so long.'

And at that admission, Freddie melted, breathlessly telling him how much she loved him while frantically tearing him out of his jeans in a generous invitation that Zac greeted with all the potent virility he could demonstrate. Freddie showered him with love and he never tired of her warmth.

'I think we should have a marriage blessing to make up for our catastrophic wedding day,' Zac told her afterwards, lying with Freddie wrapped in bliss in his strong arms. 'I've also torn up the pre-nup agreement. It wasn't fair enough to you and you signed it under duress.'

They both had a healthy appetite by the time they joined the barbecue. Zac was mobbed by the kids because he always played with them and expectations ran high.

'Freedom was never this much fun,' Zac told her before he ran off to play football with Eloise and Jack.

And with a contented sigh, Freddie cradled Antonella and sat with the new family she had gained, while marvelling in Zac's energy levels, because he had travelled for hours to get back in time for his daughter's birthday. But then that energy went into everything Zac did, she conceded, including his persistent pursuit of her. And she couldn't stop smiling at the acknowledgement that what had most annoyed her about Zac when they first met was truly his saving grace.

* * * * *

If you enjoyed
Da Rocha's CONVENIENT HEIR
you're sure to enjoy the first two parts of
Lynne Graham's
VOWS FOR BILLIONAIRES *miniseries*

THE SECRET VALTINOS BABY
CASTIGLIONE'S PREGNANT PRINCESS

And as part of the WEDLOCKED! *miniseries*

CLAIMED FOR THE LEONELLI LEGACY
HIS QUEEN BY DESERT DECREE

All available now!

#3633 CROWNED FOR THE SHEIKH'S BABY
One Night With Consequences
by Sharon Kendrick

Sensible Hannah never expected to attend a glamorous party with Sheikh Kulal. A searing kiss leads to an incredible night—and shocking consequences! Now Kulal will claim his heir by making Hannah his desert queen!

#3634 THE SECRET THE ITALIAN CLAIMS
Secret Heirs of Billionaires
by Jennie Lucas

Cristiano is furious that Hallie hid the consequences of their hot night, and demands she marry him! Their passion is still powerful... but Hallie wants a real family. Will seduction be enough to secure Cristiano's legacy?

#3635 THE BRIDE'S BABY OF SHAME
Stolen Brides
by Caitlin Crews

Sophie never challenged her arranged marriage. Until one secret night with Renzo leaves her pregnant! Renzo *will* legitimize his child—even if it means stealing Sophie from her own wedding to make her *his* bride!

#3636 INHERITED FOR THE ROYAL BED
by Annie West

After liberating inherited concubine Lina, powerful ruler Sayid is shocked by her transformation from naive to irresistible! Sayid's never wanted anyone more but can only offer a brief affair. Will Lina accept a week in his bed?

#3637 HIS MILLION-DOLLAR MARRIAGE PROPOSAL
The Powerful Di Fiore Tycoons
by Jennifer Hayward

Lazzero needs a fake fiancée to win a business deal. He offers to absolve Chiara's father's bankruptcy, *if* she wears his ring! But with their explosive attraction, soon Lazzero wants Chiara as his—for good!

#3638 TYCOON'S FORBIDDEN CINDERELLA
by Melanie Milburne

Lucien refuses to indulge in love, but delectable Audrey tests his control! Her shy innocence holds an enticing appeal. When scandal forces them together, Lucien proposes a temporary solution to their cravings—delicious surrender!

#3639 BOUND TO HER DESERT CAPTOR
Conveniently Wed!
by Michelle Conder

Certain that Regan has information on his sister's disappearance, Sheikh Jaeger steals her away to his palace. But when beautiful, defiant Regan accidentally causes a media storm, to resolve it Jaeger *must* marry her!

#3640 A MISTRESS, A SCANDAL, A RING
Ruthless Billionaire Brothers
by Angela Bissell

For Xavier, seducing stunning Jordan is a calculated risk. He's convinced their fire will soon burn out. But when their affair's exposed, there's just one option—bind Jordan to him permanently!

"I can see you are not asleep" came a familiar voice from much too close. "It is best to stop pretending, Sophie."

It was a voice that should not have been anywhere near her, not here.

Not in Langston House where, in a few short hours, she would become the latest in a long line of unenthused countesses.

Sophie took her time turning over in her bed. And still, no matter how long she stared or blinked, she couldn't make Renzo disappear.

"What are you doing here?" she asked, her voice barely more than a whisper.

"It turns out we have more to discuss."

She didn't like the way he said that, dark and something like lethal.

And Renzo was here.

Right here, in this bedroom Sophie had been installed in as the future Countess of Langston. It was all tapestries, priceless art and frothy antique chairs that looked too fragile to sit in.

"I don't know what you mean," she said, her lips too dry and her throat not much better.

"I think you do." Renzo stood at the foot of her bed, one hand looped around one of the posts in a lazy, easy sort of grip that did absolutely nothing to calm Sophie's nerves. "I think you came to tell me something last night but let my temper scare you off. Or perhaps it would be more accurate to say you used my temper as an excuse to keep from telling me, would it not?"

Sophie found her hands covering her belly again, there beneath her comforter. Worse, Renzo's dark gaze followed the movement, as if he could see straight through the pile of soft linen to the truth.

"I would like you to leave," she told him, fighting to keep her voice calm. "I don't know what showing up here, hours before I'm meant to marry, could possibly accomplish. Or is this a punishment?"

Renzo's lips quirked into something no sane person would call a smile. He didn't move and yet he seemed to loom there, growing larger by the second and consuming all the air in the bedchamber.

He made it hard to breathe. Or see straight.

"We will get to punishments in a moment," Renzo said. His dark amber gaze raked over her, bold and harsh. His sensual mouth, the one she'd felt on every inch of her skin and woke in the night yearning for again, flattened. His gaze bored into her, so hard and deep she was sure he left marks. "Are you with child, Sophie?"

Don't miss
THE BRIDE'S BABY OF SHAME,
available July 2018.

And the first part of the **STOLEN BRIDES** *duet,*
KIDNAPPED FOR HIS ROYAL DUTY by Jane Porter.

Available now
wherever Harlequin Presents® books and ebooks are sold.

www.Harlequin.com

HPEXP0618

HARLEQUIN *Presents.*

Coming next month, the first of three special *SECRET HEIRS OF BILLIONAIRES* stories by Jennie Lucas!

Hallie, Tess and Lola are all pregnant with billionaires' babies when they meet in New York City. They all have one thing in common: they haven't told any of the powerful fathers!

In *The Secret the Italian Claims*, Cristiano Moretti is furious that Hallie hid the consequences of their hot night together. He will not inflict his own childhood abandonment on his son, and demands that Hallie marry him. Soon they realize the passion between them is as powerful as ever…but when all Hallie wants is a real family, will Cristiano's seduction be enough to secure his legacy?

The Secret the Italian Claims
Available July 2018

Tess and Prince Stefano's story
The Heir the Prince Secures
Available September 2018

Lola and Rodrigo's story
The Baby the Billionaire Demands
Available November 2018

HPBPA0618